Praise for
Caroline Macon Fleischer

"*A Play About A Curse* brilliantly showcases Macon Fleischer's gifts as both a novelist and a playwright. It's a gripping hybrid narrative about ambition, betrayal, and jealousy, encouraging us to contemplate the timeless question: 'What good is it to gain the whole world but lose our very soul?'"

— Loy A. Webb, playwright of *The Light*

"With precise storytelling and a wild blending of forms, Caroline Macon Fleischer amplifies the envy, pride, wrath, and lust bubbling beneath creative collaboration. *A Play About A Curse* swims through both the psychological acuity of Susan Choi's *Trust Exercise* and the sinister chill of Fleur Jaeggy's *Sweet Days of Discipline* on its way toward deeper and stranger waters."

— Martin Seay, author of *The Mirror Thief*

"I loved this strange, often disturbing, sometimes funny chimera of a novel... Memorable, queasy, highly recommended."

— Juan Martinez, author of *Extended Stay*

"A dark, spiraling descent into the fractured mind of an artist, desperate to be seen. Caroline Macon Fleischer has created something both beautiful and unsettling. This book lingers like a nightmare. What happens when the mentor becomes the muse? A must-read for fans of *Black Swan* and other psychological horrors with teeth."

— Daniella Pineda, actor in *Jurassic World: Fallen Kingdom* and writer

"In the dust of an old building, the floorboards vibrate, a curtain draws, a scrim passes over, and out slips Caroline Macon Fleischer's genre-agnostic novel, *A Play About A Curse*. Insidious mentor-mentee relationships take center stage, trading a theatre of absolution for some psychotic bliss. Heralded by the author's hallucinogenic prose and cutting dialogue, this is a story of players cleaved from a worldly realm, flung from their obsessions, chasing the myths of their own making."

— Lucas Baisch, playwright

"*A Play About A Curse* is as propulsive as it is sui generis. Macon Fleischer's ability to crawl inside the unraveling brain of its narrator creates a journey so addictive the reader becomes an actor in the play, which is as much about envy as it is about a descent into madness."

— Eliza Bent, writer and performer

"*A Play About A Curse* is deliciously malicious. A young graduate, feeling unduly jilted by her beloved playwriting professor, trades her own humanity to master her master and sends her teacher tumbling into a whirling pool of madness. Caroline Macon Fleischer's acrobatic prose and genre-crossing storytelling is a seductive swirl of theatrical invention, wicked psychological horror, and pure pop culture pleasure. *A Play About A Curse* is an uncanny and chilling dip into the corrupted contours of the human heart, delightfully Shakespearean in scale."

— David Catlin, writer and director of
Lookingglass Alice

A Play About a Curse

Caroline Macon Fleischer

HORROR

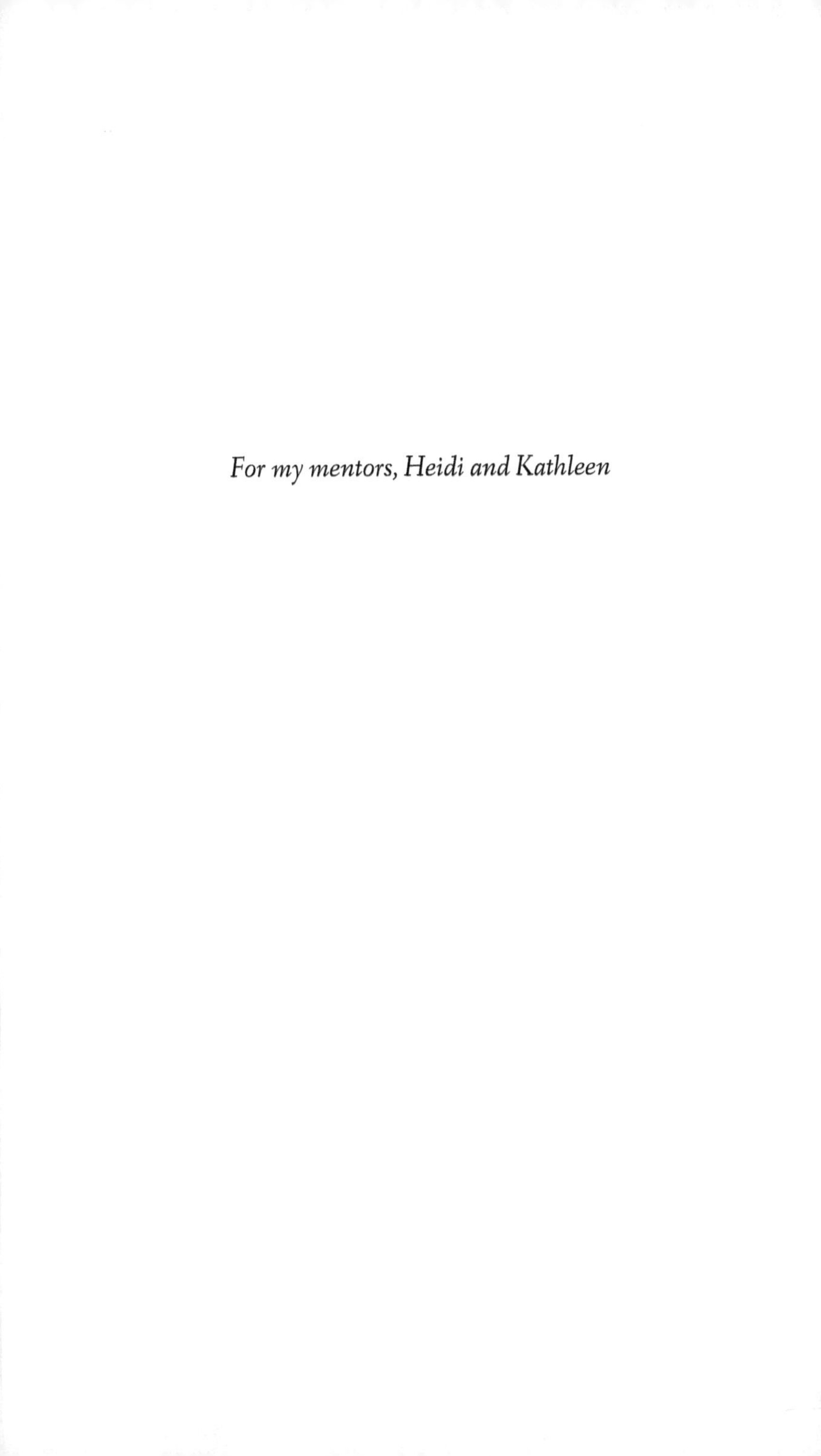

For my mentors, Heidi and Kathleen

CAROLINE MACON FLEISCHER

Presents

A Play About A Curse

Produced by CLASH Books

Characters

Corey . . . . The Mentee. 20s. Female
Maxine . . . . The Mentor. 40s. Female
Mélusine . . . . The Clairvoyant. 70s. Female
Daniel. . . . . The Artistic Director. 30s. Male

Settings

Act I: Dallas, Texas
Act II: Chicago, Illinois
Act III: Annecy, France

Production

This play includes three acts with two interludes.

A Play About a Curse

ACT I: DALLAS

ACT I: PROLOGUE

My mentor's existence would forever eclipse mine. I met her when I was a freshman in theatre school. She taught my first playwriting class. From then on, she wrote my recommendation letters and sent me home through the weeks with recordings of her favorite productions. I didn't finish any projects without her unrivaled feedback, written in signature green ink in the margins. She never missed a thing.

She was my favorite teacher. My mentor. Max.

From a grand perspective, I was a passionate young nobody, and she was the critically acclaimed Maxine Due, an award-winning playwright, scholar, and one of the few living main characters in the American theatre. And a force, at that. She paid no mind to my insignificance. There was no doubt I was her favorite right back.

It's not that I was a talented student, although I was that, too. There was something else. Some strange, uncomfortable feeling. Undefinable but unmistakable. Energies, pheromones, call it what you will, but neither of us wanted it. Eventually, the feeling grew into an enormous planet we both mistook as the other person's problem. But she was wrong, and I was right. The larger it got, so did my fear. Then resentment. Then anger. I'd get lost behind it if I didn't act fast.

This is a play about a curse because I made it so.

But before that, she took me out to dinner on the night of my graduation to celebrate.

Blackout.

The End of the Prologue.

ACT I: SCENE I

Maxine took me to one of those rare restaurants that accounts for every detail. Vintage tea towels, ceramic red ramekins, cheeses, and jams spread across boards like art. The place was packed, but I had an easy feeling. The decor was an homage to old fairy tales—magical, dark, and creepy if you squinted close enough.

I wonder if Maxine knew how important that was to me. When she was my teacher, I viewed her as a pillar in the distance, a place to walk toward where I knew I'd belong. Finally, someone I could go to shows with, split the check with, and share my opinions about art. All my life, I'd longed for that sort of connection. Nothing else mattered.

Somewhere inside, I knew putting Max on a pedestal would set me up for disappointment, but I couldn't adjust expectations. I hadn't fit in naturally with the college kids, feeling like my perspective was limited to behind the table and never in the moment. I was decently liked and respected for my work but not seen as a social being. In class, they told me my talent was one-of-a-kind, but they didn't invite me to weekend parties. Much of that was due to my own broken volition.

But there I sat. Raw. An antique chair at a French restaurant. I wore my best outfit for the occasion, a dress with a checkerboard print. I had the frame of a muscular boy, and that night, I felt really pretty. I put on a smidge of makeup, the only makeup I owned, a single tube of red lipstick. Buttons moved down my chest and stomach in a straight, dotted line. Usually, I wore flats, but the occasion demanded strappies. A meticulously chosen costume. She'd have no choice but to be my friend.

The chances of a meaningful connection with Max seemed to favor me. The restaurant's aura was spellbinding, and the menu felt smooth and cool in my hands—it was on fresh, clean, cardstock paper. While I read over the details, entrees passed by on their way to their tables, scents of herbs and spices trailing behind,

Maxine sat across from me, half her black hair twisted up and the rest curling downward, grazing the wine list as she browsed. She was confident and shapely, her curves enhanced by a subtle, flirtatious neckline. Her mannerisms were as fluid as water—controlled but carefree. Professional yet sensual, inviting but intriguingly guarded, a consistent lack of shame. She looked up at me over her reading glasses and smiled, squinting her eyes in the way only she did.

Max was a magnet for the gaze. The male gaze and the gaze of anything with eyes. Even the eyes in paintings at museums would follow her. I was sure of it. And it wasn't because of her appearance, although that was good, too—it was her striking demeanor. She vacuumed up the energy of every room where she went.

That night, her presence was extra soul-sucking, with her sangria-colored lipstick that she'd smudged softly on her brown cheeks and eyelids—simple, crisp, dewy. I basked in it, admiring it, and landed in the moment of our European bistro fantasy.

So fancy, Maxine mouthed to me, and I widened my eyes in agreement. Even though I felt classless in her presence, I appreciated how excitable she was and how easily impressed she was. Her enthusiasm for the restaurant's presentation was contagious. When I was with her, I felt like life was a play. She fawned over the service like we were at the Ritz, and in return, they fawned over us.

Maxine had an unusual quality that was scary as hell but always exciting. We all wanted to excel in her presence. I tried to make her love me, second-guess me, and never be able to let me go. During my first year of college, I resented this power of hers, but over time, I settled into it like an almost too-hot bath.

It wasn't just me, as I could see in the other students, her fans, readers, and audiences. No one wanted to act badly in her company. She may not react poorly, but feeling her judgment roil beneath the surface was terrifying. *Do you like it?* the server asked again and again. *Do you like it, Max?* the world wanted to know.

Copper pots hung from black iron hooks, and fine wine bottles in racks along the walls caught the light and threw it back somewhere entirely new. Ice in crystal. The fizz of sparkling water. Silver against flutes during toasts. Whenever the kitchen door swung open, a blast of fiery air and competing sensations. Garlic sizzling in oil.

Quadruple-time cadences of herbs being chopped. A snap of the oven closing.

We wanted every item.

We decided on Granny Smith apples, sweet-dried apricots, and a wheel of brie. Men in starched whites brought over tealights and glasses of wine. Every table was full of people. I was excited to graduate and felt like I deserved to celebrate. Like I belonged in a room, for once. My every desire seemed to sparkle through an open portal before me, an entryway to whatever came next.

As artists, we were the product. Our bodies, our words, our creations. The university curriculum pushed me to wonder every day, *Am I even good enough?* In the end, I had more of an answer. I wasn't a prodigy by any means, but the audience's enthusiasm showed me that theatre was very much worth pursuing post-grad. Behind me were years of artistically aimless teen-ness. Before me, I unspooled a career filled with terrifying unknowns.

At the end of my senior year, my first full-length play had a professional staged reading at a Dallas theatre. I got to direct the actors myself and was amazed by the tight-knit feeling the ensemble cultivated in only a month. Maxine hosted a Q&A after the play, which was a smash. The audience totally got it. And how they all clapped at the end! Some people turned to look at me while I waved sheepishly from the back.

I was never one for audiences, but my presence in the rehearsal room was another story. I wasn't good, I was great. Comfortable. Decisive, articulate, able to think on my feet and rewrite fast. I wrote until the reading day, determined to get the script right. The whole thing affirmed that four arduous years of art school were worth it.

Those conservatory-style programs have the rhythm of an unrelenting ritual. Drama school runs on a curriculum that is, in and of itself, a theatre of cruelty. The crunched schedules don't permit students to sleep or live fulfilling lives with relationships and hobbies. To pass was to succumb to getting locked up in a black box for days—quaking, filthy, and surviving on boxes of raisins and old granola bars.

Know that those brilliant, visceral, fleeting moments in plays were induced by deprivation and force. A Stanislavski exercise or a thrust into hell, no one would ever know. Some students suffered and became ill. Others ran for their lives toward the corporate world, signing their passions away in exchange for boredom. At least in boredom, there'd be some semblance of sanity.

I'd rather run a knife into my stomach than be bored.

Max would agree, which is why I thrived in her class.

Her classroom was a breeding ground for hysteria. She'd nod with serious confirmations as we wept and writhed on the grubby black box floor. We read plays where characters sucked out eyeballs, sliced off their ears, had sex with goats.

Maxine was a bizarre study in contrasts. The yang to the yin of her artistic practice was that she was calm, lovable, powdered, and put-together in real life. That's how she was that night, smiling wide-eyed at everything that came our way. She was ruthlessly polite to the wait-staff, even indulging our server for a wine sample even though she had her eye on a mid-priced rosé.

She leaned back and let her eyes drift to the ceiling. Above us hung a chandelier made from vintage champagne bottles. It twinkled in her dark gray irises, the unsuspecting color of sadness for someone who brought the world such beauty. I wanted the admission of her insecurities to demystify her and make her seem more grounded. No matter her mood, she still looked so sickeningly ethereal. Why couldn't I be like that?

The main course arrived. A squash pot pie and a skillet of Brussels sprouts. Steam and squash gravy poured out of the center of the pie like a bubbling brook. We savored every bite, closing our eyes and humming softly at the flavors, alone but still together. Exchanging pleasantries. She was wearing her listening face, the one most people didn't consider was a ruse.

COREY

Thank you for dinner. Also, the whole rest of it.

MAXINE

You deserve it.

COREY

Sometimes I feel like I don't.

MAXINE

Are you kidding?

COREY

To be honest, I haven't felt admiration. I don't mean from you. I mean, just life in general.

MAXINE

I get it. But listen: From day one, you showed incredible promise.

COREY

Do you think so? If it's true, it wasn't natural.

MAXINE

Stop playing like you don't know your ability. Tell me
what your play *The Worry Knot* is about.

Put on the spot, I felt like I'd never read my play.
Maxine was the queen of making me second-guess
myself. The noise in the restaurant was increasing—the
chatter getting drunker, the music getting louder. The
host dimmed the lights and lit more candles. The evening
was transitioning from dinner time to party time. The
activity overwhelmed me—instantly, I'd been transported
from restaurant to zoo. She looked exasperated and cut off
my thought:

MAXINE

Come on. It's about a passionate young woman who fears
letting that passion out. *Sometimes, the yearning is so
strong it could crack a rib.* You wrote that.

I shifted my hips tensely, flustered. Having someone
quote back a line that I wrote made me weak. I tried to
tuck the brassy lock of hair behind my ear again, even
though the haircut had cut my layers too short.

COREY

That line is pretty good.

Maxine exhaled, satisfied. I didn't respond. She put
her elbows on the table and got closer, helping the loud,
hectic room appear quieter to me.

MAXINE
Why are you so nervous?

I felt each freckle on my face turn pink. Whenever she prodded me like this, I took it as her way of reminding me I had more to learn. That I was the inferior one, the one who required growth. I was sure she didn't mean to insult me but to guide me. I could feel her flattered by my jealousy, even energized by it. She knew what she was doing.

I suspected my proud response to the compliment wouldn't last long. Maxine's usual approach was to break people down to sediment before building them back up again, with them unaware of what was happening, all the while cultivating respect and admiration.

MAXINE
Accept the compliment.

COREY
Thank you.

MAXINE
No one's born an artist! I don't care what they say. These are studiable, practicable skills. There's no mystique. That said, finding who you are in your art is tough. Sometimes,
it reveals things you didn't even know about yourself.
That part is a bit mystical, huh? All's to say, you were
hard to pry open at times. But the pearl was always there.
That's my spiel.

Beat.

Also, you worked like a monster and became the best.

COREY

Takes a monster to know one.

MAXINE

Haha. That's bad. Bad, but you're not wrong. Sometimes, when I'm with you, I feel like I'm looking in a funhouse mirror.

COREY

That makes me sound scarier than I probably am.

MAXINE

Why reserve darkness for the rehearsal room? You have a way of bringing it forth fearlessly. But as for my part, please don't take my edges too seriously. I push my students to their limits in class, but I do so with thoughtful intentions.

COREY

Thanks for sharing more from behind the scenes. It's helpful to get a complete perspective.

Beat.

I'm sorry if this is out of step, but I've wanted to ask now that school is over. Do you think we could be friends?

MAXINE

What? Of course I do!

COREY

Oh. Great! I'm sorry if I made that weird for you.

MAXINE

Not at all. On the contrary, I'm quite flattered.

COREY

Alright, so where do we start? What does that look like to
you? Is it a difficult shift?

MAXINE

No. We're already doing it right now. Sometimes, it's a
balance to adjust to. But I don't see harm in it! I'm friends
with a few former students. We'll have fun.

COREY

Wow! Okay. That's really nice.
I'm glad we're trying it, then. To a new version of us.

*MAXINE smiles squinty again, but it's almost as if she
catches herself. Something has shifted. Her expression
fades and then darkens.*

COREY

What's the matter?

Chocolate and raspberry soufflés arrived with chim-
neys of caramel smoke. Maxine grabbed a spoon and
made circles around the perimeter of the dish. I didn't
bother touching them. *What?* I repeated. *What's wrong?*
She put the spoon down and got ready to ruin my life.

ACT I: SCENE II

MAXINE
Corey, I should be honest with you. I accepted a playwriting residency in Chicago. I'm moving away from Texas. I didn't plan to leave yet, but this is exciting! I'm thrilled. You're the first person I've told. And really, I shouldn't have. It has yet to be announced, so please keep it mum.

Beat.

But per our newfound friendship, I feel bad! It's best this way for transparency. Of course, we'll be friends. But from a distance, for now.

Sadness poured over me. The feeling surprised me. I suddenly felt exposed. All the effort I put into the evening embarrassed me then. I crossed my ankles. I touched my napkin to my lip to remove the trace of lipstick.

I wanted to feel happy for Maxine, but her joy made me feel even worse. My body wouldn't cooperate with my brain, and the uncharacteristic level of emotion knocked me off balance. Against my better judgment, I felt scorned.

Maxine covered her eyes momentarily, then peeked at me. I saw something I'd never noticed before. A flicker of vulnerability, maybe even fear. Was she so secure in her decision? It didn't look like it.

Plus, why would she feel the need to hide? Was I scary? I'd given her no reason to think that I was scary. If anything, I'd been her doormat for four years, doing anything I could for her measly gold stars. She was ignorant of my proper dark side. At that point, I was barely even familiar with it. But somewhere within me, it rose like an unprecedented evil.

I didn't know what was happening. I covered my own eyes and prayed for a total system shutdown. The feelings kept bubbling up, hot, impossible to contain. Feeling like an outcast, I could hardly endure the private agony. My muscles throbbed. My joints ached. If I were a character in a Greek tragedy, some royal would call me hysterical and banish me to another island. Reading those plays in school, I couldn't relate to those characters. In a switch, I became one of them. Why there and then? Why?

I wanted to be nice. I wanted to be supportive. I didn't want our relationship to spoil, not back then. But the lid was about to pop. I couldn't take it.

COREY
No.

MAXINE
No?

COREY
You're the only thing tethering me to this artistic
wasteland.

MAXINE
Corey, I'm in shock.

COREY
How do you think I feel? You said we could be friends.

MAXINE
I know. We can, and we are. I'm so sorry. This is why I'm
telling you. I loved that you proposed a friendship. This is
no reflection of that. I knew you'd be disappointed, not
upset.

COREY
Are you kidding?

MAXINE
You're being a bit dramatic. This is exciting. We'll write to
one another. You can come for a visit. I'll show you
around. You can be like my little sister.

COREY
Don't say that. It's like you're rubbing it in my face.

MAXINE
No. No. I have no intention of coming across that way at
all. You should be proud of your diploma.

COREY

Don't patronize me. Who cares about that stupid sheet of paper?

MAXINE

I'm not patronizing you, Corey. Coincidentally, Daniel Cho, the Artistic Director of the theatre, was my former student. We've known each other for years, and he's evolved into a force of his own. If anything, take it as inspiration. That's enough for now. Let's eat our dessert, and then we'll get some air.

How could I eat dessert? I was nothing but a bullet on her to-do list. She'd always be the mentor, never a friend. She loved keeping me at a distance, just like the rest. This was only a stop on the farewell tour of her imaginary, egotistical tour bus. But what did I care? She'd shown me false authenticity, no different than how my diploma was a sham of real art.

MAXINE

Well-funded . . .Prestigious . . .Life-changing . . .

It was as if Chicago had it all, and my lack of presence made it even better. The nightmare unfolded before me. She'd rue the day she forgot my name and decided to treat me as a smudge on the floor of her dumb play.

The theatre was a cesspit, clamoring with greed. Playwrights didn't care about making friends. They only lusted after opportunity.

She was proof of it, the selfish bitch!

She was proof of those feelings of suspicion and fear,

as if some young voice of a generation would emerge from the depths and steal her success. Fine, then. I'd show her what that felt like.

She was utterly delusional. I saw how she looked at me, how we'd silently revealed the darkness of our innermost hearts. We'd entered the sort of para-romance that's unique to vaguely heterosexual women. Inappropriate, addictive, so bad, and so good. How could she? She'd be sorry when I was better than her and would come crawling back with lilies.

If I had it my way, I'd push the trap door button below her, and she'd fall, forced to shut her mouth. My face stayed down despite her many attempts at conversation. She finally got the hint and asked for the check.

ACT I: SCENE III

COREY and MAXINE are on a bench in the parking lot.

The heat didn't help. It was downright cruel. The sweat between my thighs got sticky fast. She didn't even look bothered.

My heart pulsed through my feet, stuffed in those uncomfortable strappy shoes. I took them off and ground my feet on the pavement. It was still warm after the sun had set, reorienting me.

MAXINE

We're both trying for a fresh start. We're both looking for something better. You need to see that. See it and learn this: Middle-aged women need opportunities, too. It's not all about you.

COREY

Fine. If you want to teach me, I'll bite. Why bother playing decorum? My decorum with you ends here. Can't you see I'm at a dead end? No one makes theatre here. It's a theatre desert. People catch a showing of *Chicago* before getting a photo with Big Tex and their deep-fried funnel cake.

MAXINE

Enough! I got it. Just stop.

COREY

You're mad now?

MAXINE

I'm so disappointed in you. You're acting beyond the pale.

MAXINE stands up. She pulls out a Virginia Slim and a brass lighter and holds the pack toward COREY.

COREY

Who even smokes nowadays?

Beat.

You know what? I'm glad you smoke. It's the one thing you've done tonight to show you're a human. Not some fancy fraud I'd meet at a gala.

MAXINE

Go at me where it hurts, then. You think I can't take criticism? I'll give it to you straight: You feel restless in Dallas because you grew up here. I felt the same about Chicago and left. Now I'm going back. Do you think I'm a failure by returning to my hometown? Your critiques are baseless, and frankly? Pretentious. Your problems aren't compelling. You're just bored and restless. Make friends. Get a boyfriend. There's nothing outside your work. I recognize it—look at me. Stop putting pressure on everything. It's like toxic gas for people to be around. And while I'm on it. You want another lesson?

She takes another drag.

Why do artists crowd in big cities? People in Texas are just as apt and desiring of art. They love it. That's why I moved here. And god dammit! I shouldn't have to give you lessons. I'm not your Mr. Rogers. I wanted to be friends, too.

COREY
You're right. You're not. You're a two-faced snake.

MAXINE
Alright. I'm a snake. We'll take space, then.

Beat.

But know that I'm always a call away.

There was nothing more to say. I couldn't bear standing with Maxine any longer, so I started walking away, my sandals still in my hands and the concrete warm beneath my feet.

At theatre school, we often returned to the idea that all art is violence. In our first textbook for Professor Due's class, the director, Anne Bogart, defines violence as decisiveness. Being decisive is violent. Articulating a decision is violent. Choice is an act of violence, one that destroys other possibilities. Art was violent, and so I was violent. If Maxine wanted to be scared of me, my choices would follow suit.

She didn't call out after me. She didn't follow me.

I don't know how long she sat on the bench. For forever, I guess. I didn't look back. For all I know, she's on another timeline and still sitting there.

ACT I: SCENE IV

COREY *sprints along a busy street.*

As soon as I disappeared from her sight, I started running. I ran as fast as possible, faster than I'd ever run. I clutched my strappy sandals and ran barefoot, powered by fury, desperate to exorcise myself from the sick rage that thrashed inside of me.

After running for so long, my feet started to bleed. There are few walkable sidewalks in Dallas. I'd been darting across scattered patches of cement and dirt, sticks in the grass, glass, debris, and streets cracked by construction work. My body throbbed and ached. I ran until I couldn't breathe.

COREY *runs out of breath. She ends up at a glowing, violet-lit strip mall.*

The glory of a pedestrian precinct. Around me, the pinks and whites of business signs flashed and blinked.

Everywhere I looked, old neon letters burnt out, spelling imperfect words. A snow cone stand in the parking lot was closed for the night, its chipping paint and nail-and-hammer construction like a dark house of sticks. I couldn't imagine going for coconut and cream or a piña colada. The whole world looked confusing.

I held my hands over my head to catch air. Finally, peace. As my pulse descended, the endorphins rose. My internal world started to open again. With every breath, senses reawakened with new clarity. An alternate reality had replaced the city I knew. I liked this version better.

The run refreshed my senses. The strip mall became a museum of oddities. Usually, when I drove past, the shops got lost in a blur. Now, each felt framed like its own unique entity. I pondered them, my pain gone euphoric. In a state of newfound zen, all the most mundane places stood as points of intrigue.

I strode, starting at one end of the mall and tracing the maze. I peered into the windows and saw whatever family ran this and that—who made donuts, handed out Bibles, and sold bongs.

I'd almost forgotten about Maxine until I reached the violet-lit sign that said CLAIRVOYANT. It was the only one with the letters still intact. The sign felt novelty, almost gimmicky. At that point in my life, I'd tried what felt like everything to combat my traumas and tribulations. Therapy, meditation, journaling. Maxine's level of betrayal was next level. It deserved a green light on a new avenue. Maybe only a fortune teller could understand how diminished I felt. I felt like I was about to walk into some sacred church.

Emotional music swelled from inside—muffled vinyl crackling beneath string instruments, a woman crooning in French. I couldn't understand the words but felt their passion and put both hands over my heart.

The music captured everything I felt about Maxine. Intrigue, darkness, confusion, and addiction. It pulled me in like an overture.

ACT I: SCENE V

The clairvoyant's den.

A hanger of chimes, amethyst, and aquamarine swung lightly at the whoosh of the door. A cat sat curled on a cushion in the foyer, where soft lines of smoke curled from a brass incense pot. Scents of woods, petals, and spices were in a haze, nearly impossible to see. Beyond the cat, I couldn't see a soul, only the faint orange glow of a lamp.

The record's sound came from the back, behind an archway draped with scarves. I realized now that someone back there was singing along gorgeously, precisely on the pitch, nearly indistinguishable from the star in the recording.

COREY
Hello?

The singing stops. The figure of a woman becomes evident in the back. Enter Mélusine, pulling on a shawl and ruffling her hair.

MÉLUSINE

Hello. Welcome. I hope I didn't keep you waiting.

COREY

No. I've never been to a psychic. Do people just walk in? I've always wanted to come to one but didn't know how.

MÉLUSINE

This is exactly how! You arrive.

The cat meandered to her and rubbed its nose along her calves. The woman's feminine warmth was very Texan, but she had a bit of a French accent that turned her sentences downward toward the end. Her soft smile was wrinkled, and her cheeks were round and red. I didn't know why, but I felt I should apologize.

COREY

I'm sorry.

MÉLUSINE

Whatever for? This is what I do. I'm glad you're here. Better late than not late—that's what I say. I hate being early. It makes everyone uncomfortable. I'm Mélusine. You may call me Mel if you like. I like both just the same.

COREY

I'm Corey. I don't have a nickname.

MÉLUSINE

I'm happy I caught you. I considered closing early tonight,
but a whisper told me not to. I should have known it
would be you. I'm psychic, after all.

Her self-referential jokes put me at ease. We shook
hands. I took the clairvoyant in, mesmerized by her
sensual nature at such a mature age. I didn't know many
mature women, but it felt like a rare trait. Mélusine radiated like an otherworldly creature.

I looked curiously at her menu of services. The
descriptions were scripted carefully on a portable
blackboard. Chalkboards always excited me, making
me feel like I was about to learn something new. Decorated with hand-drawn stars, the lavender chalk writing
said:

* SINGLE CARD TAROT *
READING YOUR DAY

* THREE CARD TAROT *
ASK ANY QUESTION

* PALM READING *
YOUR PAST

* PSYCHIC READING *
YOUR PRESENT

* FORTUNE TELLING *
YOUR FUTURE

* CURSE *

My eyes lingered on the final item, the curse, the only item without an explanation. I turned my attention back to Mélusine. A small, fragile seashell hung delicately on a gold chain below her neck.

COREY
I love that. Is it real?

MÉLUSINE
The seashell or the gold?

She flashes a vast smile with sharp teeth.

Both are real. My family and I lived at Lake Annecy in France. I picked this one up as a girl and still have it. It was my favorite.

I liked that her favorite was relatively ordinary and a little bit rough. It evoked those attachments of girlhood, those feelings of wonder that came for no reason. A translucent shade of green had a way of capturing the light.

COREY
You're a beautiful singer, too.

MÉLUSINE
Per Lake Annecy, as myth would have it, my ancestors came from the water. We're in the family of Sirens. The Mélusine is a close cousin. Still luring in the unsuspecting and eating them. An added perk is that we're snakes.

MÉLUSINE chuckles.

Don't worry, love. I didn't call you here to eat you. I've
never eaten anyone. I prefer to do my work covertly,
behind the scenes.

COREY
Understood. What brought you to Dallas?

MÉLUSINE
I followed a man. A tourist came to Annecy and stole my
heart. He sang with his Texas twang and strummed an
acoustic guitar. He was gorgeous. He bought us a house
by White Rock Lake in Dallas, and I followed his beck
and call. He loved me for years, then met someone
younger. I've lived in that house in White Rock ever since.
Enough about him. I try, with all my might, to forget.
Where are your shoes? I'll get you some slippers and
make some iced tea.

MÉLUSINE gestures to a purple velvet chair. COREY
sits.

Nothing seemed to surprise her, which put me at
ease. Mélusine exuded spiritual nurturing, the sort I'd
wanted from Maxine, who deprived me of it instead.
Mélusine tinkered about hospitably, sparse lavender high-
lights shimmering through gray hair. Everywhere I
looked, there was something to see. Diagrams of the brain,
the chakras, and the kundalini spine snake hung on navy
blue walls.

She opened a glass cabinet showcasing snow globes,

coins, and other relics from her travels. At the top, an entire row was dedicated to jars of homebrewed teas. She brought a few to me to smell. I inhaled each jar: deep toasted coconut, sweet elderberry, raspberry, and licorice. I decided on raspberry.

MÉLUSINE

I love that one. Let me make it for you, and let's talk about why you're here. I sense pain in you, so we should get right to it. You can tell me everything.

COREY

Pain puts it lightly. It's consuming. I'm jealous of my mentor. I'm crazy. I don't know why it hurts me so much.

MÉLUSINE

You're not crazy. What makes you jealous?

COREY

Where do I start? I'm a playwright. She's a wonder of the American canon. Throughout school, she felt inaccessible, strict, or cut off from something. Then, at dinner tonight. . . We had the best time, but I couldn't stop thinking about how annoying she was about everything. It's hard to put my finger on why. It's like hating Anne Hathaway, you know, what does that accomplish? Anyway, amid all this crap, the final cherry is that she was positioned for some hoity-toity opportunity in Chicago, and she has the perfect chance to bring me along. To start me off in a new light as her friend. To launch my career. Well, she said no! It was selfish. She's only thinking of herself.

*MÉLUSINE mixes the tea into powdered sugar and ice,
then hands it to COREY.*

COREY
This is perfectly sweet. Tastes like a homegrown Texan
made it.

MÉLUSINE
When in Rome.

MÉLUSINE pauses and closes her eyes, thinking.

Listen. I understand the profound impact this dilemma
with your mentor has on you. Suffering is heavy on your
heart. So heavy, you see, only dark magic might relieve it.
If we work together, we can place a hell of a curse.

COREY
Dark magic? As in, evil?

MÉLUSINE
Well, let's look at your situation. You know you're guilty,
too, right? In society's eyes, I mean. We're not supposed to
want to be better than other women, most especially not
those who taught us. But sometimes we do. Sometimes we
are. Sometimes we want their suffering. It's better to be
honest.

COREY
But this isn't a real problem. I could never be like her.
Never be as good as her. Never be as beloved. Sure, I

want all that. I want to be recognized by strangers in a bar
—and not in a famous way, just in the way that I'm seen
for what I do by other people who do it, too. Fame in the
nichiest sense. People who appreciate art.

COREY tears up but laughs, too.

MÉLUSINE
You're your own limitations. Your damaged self-worth is
sabotage. Why do you think you couldn't be better? Let's
start there. That is a broken thing to say.

COREY
What am I supposed to do? Make a wish? I don't know if
this is even real, no offense.

*COREY gestures to the room around her. MÉLUSINE
nods empathetically.*

MÉLUSINE
Clairvoyance?

COREY
I don't want to be rude. Is this a hoax?

MÉLUSINE
I will show you how it isn't.

COREY
So, I make a wish. What then?

MÉLUSINE
That depends. What is your wish?

A gut feeling came to me like an orgasm and an earthquake in one. The candle lights flickered. The linoleum tiles on the floor seemed to shift and sway like waves. Like I was on acid or possessed, and the wish rose from my ribcage and exited my mouth.

COREY

I wish I were better than Maxine. I wish I was better than Maxine in every single way.

Mélusine came in close to me, as close to me as she could, and pressed her forehead against mine. Her baby hair was soft, and her breath smelled like clove cigarettes and spearmint.

MÉLUSINE

Mentor and mentee relationships are complicated. You may not see it, but I'm sure it's tough for her to be a cheerleader. She isn't dumb—it's not a lucrative industry, the arts. It can be, but only for a lucky few.

COREY

It keeps me awake at night.

MÉLUSINE

Maxine is one of the lucky few. But you can join her.

COREY

I'm afraid there isn't room for me.

MÉLUSINE

Tsk tsk. Your broken self-image is more powerful than

your jealousy. We can't fix this until you are aware of it.
Admit it.

COREY

You're right. I hate myself, okay? It doesn't feel good.

MÉLUSINE

It sounds like Maxine's had her time, whereas you haven't
even arrived. What a great time she had. Now, there is
room for you to do the same. You need to keep making
theatre. You need it to heal.

*MÉLUSINE places her hands over COREY's ears and
presses her forehead against COREY's. They breathe in
synchrony. MÉLUSINE gives COREY a hand mirror.*

MÉLUSINE

I want you to look at yourself, your gorgeous, unique,
unmatchable self, but while you do so, I want you to give
me a mental picture of your professor. Think beyond her
appearance. What's an unforgettable detail?

COREY

She smells like jasmine.

MÉLUSINE

That's perfect. The curse doesn't work without the
personal touches of who the person is in the physical
world. Anything sensory helps the spell to take effect.

Mélusine gathered two perfume bottles, one of
jasmine oil and a second labeled as French lake water.
Once the jar was full, she dropped a seashell into the

liquid and stirred it. She twisted on the lid. She asked for another detail about Maxine, one related to a color. I looked back in the mirror and thought for a moment. Behind me, a mystical green cloud appeared, invented by imagination. I told her Maxine wrote in a green pen.

Mélusine grabbed a tall green candlestick from a rainbow set. She guided it along the lid of the jasmine and freshwater jar until it was sealed with a pop. Then, she handed me a write-in label and a black marker. I wrote MAXINE DUE and stuck it onto the jar.

Seeing Maxine's name spelled out in the context of the magical den, my interest in the ritual transformed into desire. I felt inspired by how this lovely woman integrated and embraced her shadows. I'd been catastrophizing my self-hatred. What if there was another way to look at the world? I saw a new, twisted reality where I could be one with the alchemists, the fortune-tellers, the witches, and the soothsayers.

MÉLUSINE

Now, hold the jar in front of the mirror so you know it's been preserved in your image.

I did as I was told and glanced into my eyes there, what I hoped would be the last vision of my self-hatred. Then, worldly concerns took hold. I didn't have much money.

COREY

How much does it cost?

MÉLUSINE

There is no monetary value but a critical spiritual one.

That said, I need to get something in return. You must promise me that, once the curse has run its course, you will travel to Lake Annecy and deliver something to feed the Mélusine who lives there.

COREY

How will I know what to bring?

MÉLUSINE

Trust your instincts, and you will know. I hope you will be generous. There is only so much I can give on my own. Remember the little details, as I said before. The banal technicalities of being a woman will help offset the curse's transience. The more specific, the better.

COREY

I'm desperate. Anything to keep my dream alive. I promise. You can take my word as contract.

MÉLUSINE

It's a deal. Thank you for trusting me with this, sincerely, from the bottom of my heart.

Maxine could never have known about this world—her darkness wrapped up in art and inauthenticity. It was all a pony show. A clairvoyant's den would be a subject for her to research and try to execute with corroborating details. But as with all theatre, it would miss the mark of the genuine. She wouldn't dare to experience it firsthand.

Mélusine, in contrast, was nothing but truth. There was nothing to pretend, nothing to stage, nothing to hide. The door to her heart was open, and I gladly walked inside. She wore an affectionate, concerned expression.

She closed the window, drew the curtains, and locked the door.

MÉLUSINE

Let's begin, dear. How will we be eating Maxine today?
Unconditional love is a force to be reckoned with, but
we'll restore what's been broken for you in no time.

ACT I: SCENE VI

Mélusine reached for my hands, which felt cold and bony in her warm palms. I instinctively closed my eyes. Eyes closed, I could smell the fragrance of her hair from the waves cascading over her shoulders.

With both hands secure in Mélusine's, I drifted from reality, comfortably hypnotized by nostalgia. The burst of a ripe cherry tomato. The speed of going farther and faster down a driveway on roller skates. A cluster of white and pink flower buds floating in a birdbath. My grandmother teaching me to make peach pie. The pie getting burnt on the first try. The second try being okay. What had people been so afraid of with psychics? This was nothing but nice.

Still, my confidence dwindled. felt watched. I opened my eyes.

COREY
I'm sorry. I don't know what to do.

MÉLUSINE
That's okay. Ease your mind. Embrace the discomfort. Be open to possibilities. Allow all the unknowns to feel good. Every possibility is a pleasure. You said you're a playwright? Imagine walking into the fresh slate of a new rehearsal room. Find creativity and motivation in all your discomforts. Fill the space with imagination. Use it all to your advantage. But once you drop in, under the haze of the unknown, don't let yourself get distracted. Even if it feels scary, losing your trust in the process could be dangerous. This is important for you to remember because if you lose steadfastness, the curse may start to waver. The course of the curse is never perfect, but you can manage evolutions in the curse's nature by remembering your power and the intent behind the mission. Don't lose footing.

Hummingbirds were released from my stomach. I felt dangerous, exhilarated, and committed to discovering this darker realm. This was a once-in-a-lifetime chance.

MÉLUSINE dinged a single chime.

MÉLUSINE
I need nothing from you but your honesty.

COREY
I'm trying to focus. I'm on the precipice of something but can't quite reach it.

MÉLUSINE
Don't overthink. Let it feel good. Keep sinking. Trust me.

COREY
I categorically cannot relax.

MÉLUSINE
And why is that?

I wanted to point to the usual explanations artists gave in their self-victimization—that my parents' absence had stifled my growth, that graduating was confusing and tough, and that middle school was supposed to contain the hardest years of my life. Yet, my late teens prevailed in awfulness. Time had not healed me but made me perhaps even more vexed and tormented. But that evening, all those messy details felt insignificant, almost trivial.

Instead, to my surprise, I accepted that my life in a larger context had been fine. I could only pinpoint Maxine as a source of sorrow. Her success, way of doing things, and general being seemed unattainable. It sickened me so—wretched, stupid, silly me. I grieved for my lack of Max.

MÉLUSINE
Do you feel that?

COREY *swallows and nods. Her body sinks further into rest.*

Good. Let your sorrow deepen. There's no harm in it, for

now. Feel the liquid move from your tear ducts to your mind, then fall down the back of your throat.

MÉLUSINE chimes again. In the background, a faint rustling of wind and trees, the cat's sleeping purr, the grandfather clock's ticking.

Imagine the outcome you wanted, but state it to yourself in the present. State the desire as if you're experiencing it as fact.

I did what I was told, thinking: *I graduated this week. Maxine is taking me with her to a new opportunity. I'll join her in this strange field we were crazy for pursuing in the first place. Her role is to support me. She wants nothing but the best for me.*

I could feel the clairvoyant studying me still, almost like I could see through my eyelids. This time, it didn't bother me. When I manifested my desires for Max in the present, I visualized a space I'd never seen, a cold, dark hole surrounded by the peaks of mountains.

COREY

I'm confused by where my thoughts are turning. I don't see Maxine. Where am I?

MÉLUSINE

I can't interpret the specifics of your mind, only the essence. I'm not there in the setting with you. So, tell me what you see.

COREY

I'm in a place I've never seen in my life. An unplaceable
memory.

MÉLUSINE

Is anyone there with you?

COREY

No. It's just me.

MÉLUSINE

Excellent. As it should be. I'll try to keep her away for
now. We'll bring her in later. We'll breathe in rhythm to
the sound of the clock. Find your own pace that allows for
deep breathing. Let the seconds pass and use the soft
ticking as a cue. It means you're not there yet if it feels like
you've been silent too long. This will take as long as it
takes. Be patient as I observe you. I will know when you
are ready. You'll be safe, dear, I promise.

I did what she said once more, syncing as one with the
sounds around me. At first, time extended like a never-
ending tunnel. Eventually, the tunnel disappeared. Time
disappeared. Then I disappeared, too. Without the
barriers of my body, my soul spread like fog, attaching to
nothing. I realized space wasn't planets, stars, or even
blackness but a prismatic void of indiscernible color.

Then, a magnificent dark planet appeared, a planet
made of water. Music radiated from it like the Sirens'
sounds were its center of gravity. I tried to rush toward it,
but my feelings had ceased. Anger and despair still teth-
ered me back to Earth, Texas, and Maxine. The amor-
phous feeling of my soul had reverted to the ridiculous

limitations of a flailing human. My breath fell out of sync. I became constricted, gasping.

MÉLUSINE

Don't thrash like that. It will make it hurt worse.

I started to cry. My feelings wouldn't cease. Every sound from the clairvoyant's den disappeared into a vacuum. Complete stillness. A profound lack thereof.

MÉLUSINE

Open your eyes.

I did. I sat in the velvet chair. Everything looked the same, just silent. Like looking at a photograph. Nothing moved. I was alone. Where was Mélusine? Where was the cat? My thoughts buzzed. Throbbing. Dizzy. Afraid that was the end of the world as I knew it.

Then, a thunderous crack. Startled, I curled into the fetal position and plugged my ears. I winced, taking in a most fearful sight. The Earth shook, splitting the floor apart. I tried to recenter, but my efforts were futile. Mélusine's many collections slipped through breaks in the floor into darkness, splashing into great, dark water. I panicked, coughed, and clawed at my chest like I was undergoing a heart attack.

I did what she asked and didn't thrash. I channeled all my willpower to fight the automatic response to pain. I hurt as if all my bones had been broken, but I stayed still. I relented to the rubble as life collapsed all around me. The entire strip mall fell through the ground, the street-lamps, the snow cone stand, and every store swallowed up, business by business.

Then, everything was gone. I stood alone in the ruins of the parking lot. I inhaled with relief, but one final split opened beneath me. I fell in, screaming, bracing to fall into the raging sea that everything else had.

Instead, I landed in a quiet place, a shift into a scene in my memory. I was a freshman in college again. I was sure of it because I wore the short haircut I got when I was excited to start school. I faced myself in the bathroom mirror, washing my hands and smoothing out my clothes to head into Professor Due's class for the first time.

I felt insecure and nervous. I discovered the start of this embedded worry in my heart that I would never be good enough, and despite how well I cleaned myself in the mirror, the worry showed clearly on my face.

I reached into my bag for my cell phone to verify the room number. Yes, there it was—the first contact from Maxine I ever received: a welcome email signed in the emerald-green Garamond of Maxine's email signature.

My stomach leaped when I saw it again: Maxine Due | Visiting Professor of Playwriting. Under it was an italicized quote by the playwright Suzan-Lori Parks: *Every play I write is about love and distance. And time. From that, we can learn things like history.*

Throughout my four years of college, I contemplated the quote. As time passed, it reconfigured into new meanings. My understanding was initially stunted by my ripe, young age—a testament to how people seasoned over time. In retrospect, the circumstances of her choice to use it as a college professor were intriguing. It was the perfect pick for readers on the precipice of life between child and adult.

I tried to ignore my confusion about the time warp, meandering in my old skin with curiosity. I could think of no better way to start and complete my college years than with an act of rebellion. If nothing else, I hoped my visit to the fortune teller would shed some light on my future purpose, where my career would lead, and what would happen to me and Maxine.

I grabbed my backpack and walked into class. There she stood. Maxine. I saw her again, for the very first time. She embodied all I wanted to be—a casual linen pantsuit, glasses at the end of her nose, her black curls falling effortlessly down her chest. My other classmates were there, too. She circled us up for an icebreaker.

Maxine clicked along in Oxfords to the center of the circle. As she passed, wafts of her jasmine lotion floated through. She settled us in and joked in her perfect way, her charming self-deprecation, her relatability. But behind that, her presence was firm, strong, and respectable. I watched how she captivated us all, knocking her first impression out of the park, as I remembered.

Her intensity scared the class straight. From there, I started to develop my ideas based on her ideas. I failed to bring newness to the class content. This should have been my first indication that I'd never be as good as her. To an extent, I had to blame myself for my lack of originality. Maxine only ever solidified her unique ideas through her blunt, pointed teaching style.

She was inherently good at culling together resources to create something new and interesting. Knowing what I knew after deepening our relationship, I understood this as a skill she wasn't born with but had tuned in after years of practice. How could I expect myself to be better than her if all I did was emulate her process and behavior? I'd never be her, but didn't know how to be me.

This bothered me too much to admit. As badly as I wanted to find myself in those precious twisting years of young adulthood, I couldn't shake the desire to be her. She was Mozart, and I was Salieri.

She was the dazzling artist of erudition, and I was simply the follower. Even revisiting the memory in the context of the clairvoyant's den, I felt the epic power of the knowledge I was missing.

MAXINE

Please share your name, where you're from, and why you're here.

I waited in suspense as the students around me answered. The suspense traveled from my head to my hands until they shook. My heartbeat was so inconsistent that I nearly felt ill. I tucked my hair behind my cars and waited and waited. I wondered if she felt my gaze on her —if she was even real or could feel anything.

Finally, she arrived. She stood in front of me. We met eyes for the first time there, and she smiled politely. We stared for a bit longer, then she smiled, her eyes squinting as if she'd recognized me. Like she saw my soul. I almost fell in love again, but after all I'd been through, I had to stay faithful.

COREY

I'm Corey. I grew up here, in Dallas, and. . .

COREY pauses. She inhales. Her eyes widen.

I'm here to put a curse on you.

Blackout.

The End of Act I.

INTERLUDE: DANIEL

INTERLUDE: DANIEL

At rise, DANIEL's Interlude. Messages project onto the scrim. Mechanical sounds of typing punctuate the silence.

Subject: Reaching out?

Dear Mr. Daniel Cho:

You don't know me, but I'm about to change that. My name is Corey Cordele, and I'm writing to ask about the Chicago Playwriting Residency. I hear you're the artistic director in charge of the program.

My [amazing, I'm sure you know] mentor, Professor Maxine Due, told me about the residency. I hope the fact that she told me this won't bother you, as I know the program hasn't been publicly announced. She and I are close, and she told me in hopes for us to celebrate.

I just graduated from the Theatre Conservatory in Dallas. I've lived here my whole life and can't help but wonder. . .

What is the theatre scene like in Chicago? Endless talk about New York, which may even be a rivalry for you. I have a hunch that Chicago goes under the radar. I don't want Broadway accreditation for my career so much as an opportunity to be hands-on in smaller spaces. Recently, I had the privilege of working with a cast in my first-ever rehearsal room, where I got to direct my own play. It got my wheels turning about Chicago, a la storefront theatre, and maybe it could be a nice fit for me.

I know what you're thinking. I'm too young to apply for this. I get it. That's not why I'm reaching out. Moreover, I'm curious what advice you may have for a village young-ster. Chicago could be on my radar for a potential theatre move. If you have time, let me know if you have any tips. By the way, and it's not theatre-related [and sorry, I stalked, digging for your contact info], I'm also a big fan of Modest Mouse. I love the use of "Dark Center of the Universe" in *The Shipment* by Young Jean Lee. I guess it is theatre-related, after all. Isn't everything?

Sincerely,
Corey Cordele

* * *

Subject: RE: Reaching out?

Hey Corey. Thanks for writing. Funny that you should mention the [most important] mouse and that [incredible] play. I [literally, just last week] revisited it. I'd love to direct it one day. Antics for another time. You're right: I'm Team Chicago Theatre, always. It's criminally underrated. I'll get to your other questions. But say more about what you're working on.

Daniel

* * *

Subject: RE: RE: Reaching out?

Dear Daniel,

Thank you so much for writing me back, and so fast. Prayers answered! I'm always happy to meet [i.e., I live for it] another aficionado of the [undervalued punctuation mark, IMO], the aside bracket.

I'm researching Annecy, France, which you may know for the International Animation Film Festival. It's a medieval town near Geneva, in the Swiss Alps. A friend was born there and introduced me to the mythic history of Sirens in Lake Annecy. It piqued my interest because I love mermaids unpretentiously. I'm friends with Flounder and Sebastian and in reverie of the OG, Hans Chris. While I'm at it, did you see *Luca*? As you put it, antics for another time.

When I looked up the lineage of Sirens in Annecy, I fell down this crazy-fascinating rabbit hole. I'm FLOORED by the endless lore of it all. FIRST OF ALL, Annecy is a well-preserved medieval town built around a prison that's surrounded by a moat. They didn't want prisoners swimming away. The former jail still stands in the middle of a moat today. A welcome center or something, now. Creepy!

Furthermore, RE the Siren thing, the legends go deep. Some experimental artist named John Foncuberta [spelling?] installed a "historic" archaeological discovery of Siren fossils, allegedly found on the shore of Lake Annecy by a fictitious archaeologist in the late forties. Pic attached. Bonkersville levels of realism, right? I love the mortal mermaid tales. That led me further into the Mélusine, a woman under a curse that makes her half-serpent. Sorry to blab, but to answer your initial question, I'd love to continue pursuing this and eventually center it into a play. Thank you for reading if you did.

Sincerely,
Corey

* * *

Subject: RE: RE: RE: Reaching out?

Hey Corey. Can I call you?

* * *

The ring of a cellphone.
The following exchange is in voiceover, a call:

DANIEL
You have me. That's some of the craziest shit I've ever seen.

COREY

I'm like, this man is going to think I'm insane!

DANIEL

You one hundred percent are. But. Oh my god. I was up way too late digging. Did you see the one where the girl loses her lover and jumps off the waterfall at Angon? What???

COREY

Well, she didn't lose her lover. The devil made a deal with her to find him but put him in all these disguises, so it was impossible. Leave it to medieval people. A character puts on a costume that renders them unrecognizable.

DANIEL

Oh-kay, oh-kay. You're the leading scholar. I'm just a newbie on the research team. Ha ha ha. Anyway, I just wanted to tell you that.

COREY

Thanks. It's nice meeting you by phone.

DANIEL

Yeah. Hey. To answer your original question. Chicago could be good for you. Let me keep thinking about it. If something comes to mind, I'll send it your way.

The audio ends. Back to the screen, this time with the feeling of a moving train. Lights speed past as if moving through a tunnel.

* * *

Text Message from Maybe: Daniel Cho

111:08 AM: Hey! It's Daniel Cho
11:08 AM: Sorry to text. I'm on the train.

COREY
11:10 AM: Hi! I was hoping I'd hear from you.

DANIEL
11:11 AM: Lol. Look
11:11 AM: I'm also insane for this. But
11:11 AM: Can you put the Annecy stuff in a proposal?

COREY
11:12 AM: Like an outline?

DANIEL
11:12 AM: Yes. And an overview of your research
11:13 AM: Resume. Elevator pitch. Any snopsis you
might have already
11:13 AM: *synopsis

COREY
11:14 AM: I'm intrigued.

DANIEL
11:15 AM: Anything related? But formatted facy
11:15 AM: *FANCY. Ugh
11:16 AM: Fancier than me. [Scattered artist, on the go]

COREY
11:19 AM: Lol. It's humbling.
11:19 AM: Your types usually feel out of reach.

11:20 AM: Can I ask what for?

DANIEL
11:24 AM: Yes. RE: My types.
11:24 AM: I'd like to run it by the board
11:26 AM: I had this thought. Lol
11:27 AM: What if you joined Maxine and me?
11:27 AM: It's the program's first year, so I want a group that jives
11:28 AM: I'm sorry not to be more formal. Not interested in pony shows
11:28 AM: In it to make cool stuff

COREY
11:30 AM: ??? !!! [Screaming internally]
11:31 AM: I thought I was too young.

DANIEL
11:32 AM: Lol
11:32 AM: I never said that
11:33 AM: You said that

COREY
11:34 AM: Baha. I'll send it by EOD.
11:36 AM: Suspense! Omg. Let me know what they think.

DANIEL
11:40 AM: I have a feeling I'll see you in the fall

COREY
11:44 AM: Okay. No pressure!
11:45 AM: [Thank you. Thank you. Thank you.]

DANIEL

11:46 AM: I can't wait to read.

11:51 AM: Did you tell Maxine we've been chatting?

11:52 AM: She'll be stoked

COREY

12:03 PM: No, not yet!

12:05 PM: I want to surprise her. :)

DANIEL

12:10 PM: Copy. It'll be a surprise.

12:17 PM: Would you two be comfortable leasing a 2BR?

12:20 PM: That could give us more budget for readings, etc.

12:21 PM: I thought I'd ask since you're already so close.

COREY

12:22 PM: Absolutely. A dynamic adjustment, but fine.

DANIEL

12:30 PM: Amazing. Also. I'm curious:

12:30 PM: Thoughts on Modest Mouse touring now that Jeremiah Green is dead?

The screen goes dark.

Blackout.

The End of Daniel's Interlude.

ACT II: CHICAGO

ACT II: SCENE I

I hoped to find Maxine in ruins by the time I reached Chicago. Maybe she'd drop her funding contract, perhaps she'd have an accident, or maybe I'd find her incapacitated on the floor of our shared apartment.

Since I had placed the curse, euphoric vigor rushed up my spine to my skull. It was such a pleasure that I fantasized it would break my bones without pain, transforming me, shelling me from my human limitations, and releasing me into a spiritual realm.

The aftereffects of the curse were so intense that I assumed they were equally as explosive in Maxine. But hopefully, hers were launching in the opposite direction, toward suffering. In other words, as Jung put it, *No tree can grow to heaven unless its roots reach hell.*

How had she fared? I couldn't wait to see.

I arrived in early September, just as summer was fading into fall. My new confidence safeguarded me through the unknowns of the city. I traced the perplexing maze of O'Hare airport. Shuttles operated in reverse, moving backward through the tunnels. I quickly learned that the concourse to the entrance of the Blue Line trains was full of red herrings. Signs pointed around corners, to prohibited areas, to dead ends. The same upward arrow indicated going upstairs and walking ahead. In a similar double entendre, the downward arrow showed turning around and going downstairs.

Elevators led to escalators, which led to a bridge to a final escalator down. There, in the dim light of the Blue Line, almost entirely void of people except a few still inside, sleeping, I knew the code before it was taught to me. The Blue Line launched backward into the city. As we moved, I sat in the opposite direction, observing my new world like a thrilling, scary rollercoaster.

We jolted about in unpredictable patterns—from ground level to underground, then above once again—for a moment, elevated. I was dumped at a station in the heart of downtown called Jackson, where there was yet another voyage through a lower-level tunnel and onto a red line that ran below.

I couldn't access the GPS there, but it was no bother. I was busy decoding the puzzle box of Chicago, my mind ahead of my body with unprecedented clarity. With this strange, new, psychic knowledge, I arrived at the three-story building where Maxine and I would live. I made my way up flights of stairs like they were second nature and pulled the key hidden for me inside a lamp in the hallway.

I beat her there.

The place looked sturdy and mostly well-kept, with hardwood floors, plenty of windows, and the Chicago character I had imagined. A grand, mythical-looking archway extended along the ceiling, dividing the living room from the kitchen. For a two-bedroom, the space was nice. There was no dishwasher and no air conditioning—Texas blasphemy. A window AC unit sat jammed into a crooked frame.

Adjacent to the kitchen stood a masculine cabinet with doors and drawers that squeaked and were still lined with their original striped paper. The back door emptied onto a multi-tiered balcony, a swamp of crusty bug bodies and pigeon poop.

The shower walls were plastered with ceramic fish scale tiles, and the toilet still had a pull chain. The landlord had apologized for the apartment's outdatedness, but keeping it as is helped keep the rent low. I didn't mind. Soon, the building would be ripped to shreds and swapped with something unsustainably greige. Despite what sellers may want you to think, there was nothing theatrical about bad renovation. I liked it as it was.

Since I arrived before Maxine, I took over the larger bedroom near the front of the house. She could dwell in the back, where a square window looked over the back staircase and balcony.

Thuds came up the front stairwell, struggling and echoing. The unwieldy sound of bags falling and keys jingling grew more apparent with every step.

Enter MAXINE.

There she was, timid in the doorway. Sweaty. Panting. The look of a question mark on her face. She dug under her blazer, trying to check the time. Her hands were full, her tote overpacked. Coins fell from the pockets, crashing like disorganized cymbals.

I emerged to say hello, to ask about her travels. The moment I'd been waiting for, rehearsing lines and scenarios in my head. Before I could speak, she collapsed like a ragdoll over the kitchen counter.

The proof sat in disarray before me: I had no reason to doubt the curse.

My first indication that something was amiss was the lack of wafting jasmine as she entered. She also had a new mound between her neck and back. Her eyes were wild with reflective sparkles, but at the same time, dim and distant. It was hard to find her inside them, as if she were intoxicated when she wasn't. The jarring electricity of her eyes contrasted with her dolorous physical output. As she entered the room, the wind seemed to howl in despair.

All the proof I needed was neatly folded into one pile at first glance. Perfect. The curse was as real as the organs within me—protecting me as promised, giving me energy, and keeping me alive. Instinctively:

COREY

Do you need water?

MAXINE

I shouldn't have carried those bags myself. I thought I'd reorient with the city, but getting here felt like a new language I didn't know how to interpret. Like I'm missing some sort of code. I could barely board the train without second-guessing the neighborhood at every stop. I'm bone tired. How was your trip?

COREY
Nothing remarkable.

MAXINE
I'm having problems. It isn't about you, so before you get
selfish, let's get this out of the way now: When I signed
the contract and saw you on the lease, it was a jump scare.

COREY
I can only imagine.

MAXINE
You went behind my back. Then, I thought twice about it,
and you know what? I was shocked by the way you didn't
spread yourself out like a doormat in front of me. You've
grown a spine. Much more initiative than I'd seen in you.
I shouldn't bother controlling you. What's the point when
you do what you want anyway? You're a vindictive little
shit, but you advocated for yourself and showed your
capabilities. I suppose I'm proud of you. Why should I let
this ruin my opportunity?

COREY
I see. . . Thank you. So, what else has been going on?

MAXINE rolls her eyes.

MAXINE
Where do I start? I couldn't sleep for weeks and
deteriorated to a morsel. Eating crumbs, too. Inanition.
That's what it's called. Only mentioning it because I
Googled it while waiting for the TSA, who pulled my bag
and wiped it with a little strip like I'd packed a bomb. I

should have, with how things have been going! I don't mean to be insensitive. Anyway, the airplane pretzels were honey mustard, and they were terrific. Lucky me, some nearby mom had a toddler who hated them and just gave them to me. I can't remember if I brushed my teeth this morning, so you'll have to excuse me if my breath stinks. I'm having nightmares. And *oh my god*. Downright predatory. I had nightmares as a teenager, but eh, no, I really didn't, not like this. The fly-by-the-minute nature of coming home made me go berserk. It'd make more sense if my meddling parents still lived here, but they moved away and retired. I loved Texas. Leaving was more complicated than I thought. Not to be a downer. I was so excited about this, but all day, I wanted to wash down melatonin with some wine.

I watched her with my jaw dropped, in awe of her mania. Not the state I expected her to be in, but over the top. A spectacular level of drama. She practically kicked down the door with nonsense. I bit my lower lip not to laugh. I hoped the scene would be ugly but didn't foresee her wild hyperactivity. The venting. Her energy soared off the planet—not down to hell, per the Jung quote, but as high as it could go. Eventually, it'd turn right back around and smash through the surface.

Then, I focused on the evidence affixed by a gold chain around her neck. An unremarkable seashell.

COREY

Where did you get that? I love it.

MAXINE

I got it when I was a kid at Oak Street Beach.

COREY
You've never worn it before.

MAXINE
I forgot about it. I found it when I was packing. Does it look too amateur? Does it make me look dumb? You'd tell me if it looked stupid, right? Sorry. I'm out of sorts. UGH. I need to get a grip.

She reached toward her neck and clawed at the chain, rushing to the mirror to see if the accessory looked cheap. Her hands moved from the chain to her cheeks, running her fingers along lines in her face that only she could see. She poked at every pimple. I noticed her skin had been picked at, her hair over-brushed and over-sprayed and shiny in the wrong places. She flipped it over and twisted it into a messy bun. To make it go away. She pulled at her shirt, getting the fabric away from her stomach. I saw her desire to disappear inside it. She shut off the mirror light and ran away.

Amazing. She absorbed my weakness in real time. When I cut the rope, my feelings went to her. My insides quaked, emptying themselves of negativity. And, *Oh my god*, I was exultant. Prim and polished, nary a hair amiss. She was windblown, unironed, and stale from her travels. Once she caught her breath, she apologized to me after everything I'd done!

Maxine knelt before her open suitcase, wrestling with the zipper, which eventually surrendered, cutting a bit of skin off her thumb. She sucked at the blood while tossing garments over her shoulder in increasing desperation. Silks were thrown into helpless heaps. Pants, usually so carefully pressed, twisted into rope.

Her eyes returned to the bathroom, studying my outfit for the next day, hanging on a wooden hook to smooth perfectly in the humid air of the shower. A vintage gothic dress emanating the no-cares confidence of someone who knew exactly who they were.

Where is all your shit? Maxine muttered to herself. Hasty. Broken. Upending her makeup bag. Loose powder spilled onto the floor and across her palms, leaving handprints on everything she touched. Her favorite green pen rolled under the radiator. Even her signature scent seemed wrong, too sweet suddenly, cheap and candy-like, cloying in the unfamiliar space. Nearly adolescent.

She caught her reflection in the window—she thought she'd effectively hid from the mirror! She glared at herself, her hair wild, clothing rumpled like she'd slept through the plane ride, but I knew she hadn't. Behind her, the room looked like the remains of a tornado. Bags half open, shoes flying and scattering, jewelry tangling in impossible knots. A far cry from her orderly office back in Dallas, where everything had its place, and every place knew its purpose.

Her hands shook as she tried to fold a blazer. The fabric wouldn't cooperate, bunching stubbornly at the shoulders. She said she'd packed it for its elegance and revered it as a part of her power suit. Now, it looked shabby, student-like. Amateur, just as she'd feared.

She mumbled to herself in angry commands. Her voice sounded foreign in the new, strange room. She'd given hundreds of first lectures and mentored countless students. Why did this feel different? Why did her carefully curated wardrobe suddenly feel like costumes from someone else's life? Her self-hatred like taunts, chanting. She'd become unaware of her beauty, remaining youth, and charisma. She was still doing all those things but lacked sureness and confidence.

She sank onto the floor, perching, stiff at the center of chaos. Her fingers found a loose thread on her sleeve, and she twisted it about. In an instant, the old mentor and mentee hierarchies started to wrench. Our dynamic distorted like the clothes strewn around her. She tried to wipe up spilled makeup powder on bare wood with her fingers. Frustrated, she hit the ground. A first rebellion against what would become of her undoing.

I couldn't wait for the first playwriting meeting.

ACT II: SCENE II

The old parochial school.

I approached the eerie, rusted door of the parochial school. A dank, sweet smell of old hymnals and wood polish crept out from beneath it. My stomach wrung with curiosity.

I entered the ground floor, where a girl my age rose from a pile of cubicles near the entrance. She introduced herself, a name I didn't care to memorize, and led me to a stairwell to the basement. Her footsteps echoed sharply on the worn steps while mine fell muffled behind.

The girl wouldn't shut up, her voice bouncing off the concrete walls in overlapping waves. She treated me as a celebrity, in awe of me. Her chatter reverberated through the stairwell, making my head throb. The steps creaked a different note under each footfall. Cool air wafted up, carrying the unmistakable smell of holiness past its sell-by date.

A centenarian maroon rug zigzagged me into the black cavern where the playwrights met. Old coffee urns, musty hymnal pages, and decades of potluck dinners ground onto the floor. I arrived early to mark my territory, refusing to find Maxine lurking in the room.

Seeing the room for the first time gave me goose-bumps. The paint on the walls bubbled and peeled in patches, revealing layers of erased colors underneath—gold, army green, and sapphire blue. No one had bothered to renovate, save for those globby coats of paint that froze in drips.

Besides the pops of indecisive school spirit colors, the gothic feeling of the creepy old school was perfectly preserved. Even the shadows looked ancient, thick with settled dust that danced in the weak light from high windows.

I slid my sunglasses onto my head, set down my iced coffee, and stood mesmerized. Jesus loomed over me from his crucifix above the door. His face, which before I'd interpreted as an expression of pain, now looked twisted in my judgment. The failing fluorescents cast his shadow huge against the wall. His stare felt malevolent, disproving of every step.

But I didn't care what he thought. He thought I was despicable, and he wasn't wrong. I was unworthy of being there, but it didn't matter because I was there. Did I deserve it? No. Maxine should have thought twice before scorning me. I should have felt ashamed that even the son of God would harbor disdain. But I didn't.

I felt sick with glee.

I reached into my bag for some lipstick to enhance my spiritual revival.

The hideous room engrossed me. It wasn't at all how I'd imagined it. The actual theatre of the company, down the street, was so fancy it was icky. I couldn't trust it. But the workshop room. . . wow.

In new contexts, my Annecy research resurfaced vigorously. I had a seed of obsession with *The Little Mermaid*, which Disney released a few years before I was born. I thought I was Ariel, the cartoon incarnated into a human fishhood. Her luscious ginger locks validated me, inspiring my coppery hair.

I didn't relate to the character arc how I was supposed to—instead, I wanted the opposite of her wants. I hated humanity and dreamt of fishhood.

As the wise Sebastian says in the film, *The human world, it's a mess.* It was the first line in a script I identified with at a cellular level. My first text analysis. Musicals were stories plus songs—my two favorite things.

As a child, I'd chassé across the empty church parking lot to the uplifting bedlam of "Under the Sea" on my Walkman: the seashell percussion, the clam castanets, the sound of an ironic tuba, a sea snail using a conch as a wind instrument, jellyfish tentacles as a harp. The flutes —the flutes! A silverfish blowing on coral as if it were a recorder. Triangles pinging in silliness as Sebastian gets another kooky idea and kicks off another bit. Flounder spinning, getting the crap beat out of him in slapstick. Then, the cymbals smash and crash and descend into pandemonium.

Nothing like the Andersen original, with the haunted phrase, *A mermaid has no tears, and therefore, she suffers so much more.* I never understood how tears could relieve suffering in the first place. I wasn't sure that was true.

Furthermore, I wondered why mermaids would have no tears—why wouldn't the tears flow anyway, mixing with the water?

Transported to Chicago. To the mess of the human world that old crab referred to. Being there in the flesh, the mess took on a new meaning. Macabre enough to break health codes. Freaky enough to draw the best artists in the nation.

The walls breathed with all their rehearsals amidst bygone laughs and cries of Catholic schoolchildren. A row of stained-glass vignettes bordered the top of a muddy garden view. Their blue and green hues scattered across my arms, striped with rain. Everything was dim and cold. I grinned.

Damp cardboard boxes of old church programs lined the walls, their pages wavy with basement moisture. The air was shallow. A bathroom fan rattled down the hall-way, where a barely open door teased freakish, flickering light. The cornucopia of school scents included mildewed songbooks, candle wax, and whatever decades of recipes got scattered across folding tables at potlucks.

A string of Christmas lights turns on. Several of the bulbs are burnt out. A male voice.

DANIEL
Ugh! I just tested these.

Enter DANIEL. He sees her, and they freeze. They lock in.

Hi. Corey. I didn't mean to startle you. I thought I was the first one here.

COREY
Nice lights.

DANIEL
More like tacky. I don't know why half the bulbs are out.

COREY
Chronic brokenness is the charm of such a thing.

DANIEL
Not tried enough, not true enough. Forgive the space. I know it's a little eccentric.

COREY laughs.

COREY
Hi.

DANIEL
Hi. Wow. I'm excited to meet you in person.

COREY
You, too.

They hug. The pop of static shock.

DANIEL
Sorry. This windbreaker has a way of conjuring lightning when it rains. You don't look like your picture.

COREY
I'm not very photogenic.

DANIEL
I can see that. No offense.

Daniel hopped through the room without hesitation, as I'm sure he'd done a thousand times before. I watched from across the room as he set down grocery bags full of snacks. Daniel. There. Close but out of reach.

The basement air hung thick with history—decades of rehearsals, prayers, and confessions. Every surface seemed to hold memories: scuff marks from countless shoes, initials carved into wooden panels, old programs wedged between radiator fins. Daniel moved through it all like a conductor through his orchestra, each gesture precise and purposeful.

I helped without asking. We mixed about in sync—precise, coordinated, optimal. When we stood face to face, we were at eye level. Our matching heights surrendered me. He was small but strong from years of circus work, which I'd inspected on the internet. Calluses on his palms detailed memories of handstands, trapezes, and silk knots.

His movements had a performer's grace—the kind you can't learn in theatre school. They came from years of trusting your body to catch you, to hold you suspended above an audience. I studied how his shoulders moved under his shirt, imagining the muscle memory of countless aerial acts written into his bones.

A decades-old coffee maker dripped somewhere in an adjacent room, its burnt aroma mixing with chalk dust. The light switches made loud, mechanical clicks that almost sounded like hiccups. When trucks drove past, the fragile walls of the basement shook, making the Christmas lights sway slightly.

Each vibration seemed to pulse between us, an invisible thread pulling tighter. The basement's dampness made everything feel more intimate and contained, as if we were sealed away in our pocket universe, safe from the world above.

He got a broom and dustpan and went to work on the floor. Once that was finished, he stood back and eyed the room with the unrivaled focus of an artistic director. Every space he entered required balance. Violence.

I watched his eyes scan the room, seeing past what was there to what could be. This was his magic—not the showy performance tricks, but this quiet alchemy of transforming spaces. He could look at peeling paint and water stains and see possibilities.

Even the untended vending machine in the corner transformed into a set piece. The brightly colored buttons radiated points of interest onto the walls. The room radiated with possibility. No wonder Daniel was so bad at texting. There he was, wherever he was.

The fluorescent lights buzzed overhead like distant insects, casting strange shadows in the corners. Everything felt slightly unreal, slightly enchanted. Each moment seemed to stretch and compress simultaneously, like underwater or in a dream.

I loved him.

The machine was so old it only required a quarter. I bought him a pack of Pixy Stix and walked them to him. The way he looked at me confirmed what I'd hoped. We existed in a private network, somehow, with our correspondence. In the third dimension, it was apparent that this secret currency was still transferred between us. I opened one of the Pixy Stix, sprinkled a little into my palm, and blew it into a cloud.

The sugar dust caught the Christmas lights, sparkling like theatrical snow. We both watched it drift and settle for a moment, adding another layer to the basement's endless strata of memories.

ACT II: SCENE III

*The parochial school. DANIEL pulls a folded sheet of
notebook paper from his pocket. A welcome monologue:*

DANIEL

Bear with me today for any nervous emotion. I can't
overstate what this means to me. No pair in the world is a
better fit than you. I'll share the story of our journey here
today and explain why this union is kismet.

Beat.

The day I received the oracle, something about its
understated nature made everything else feel heightened
and significant. The letter arrived without a postmark or
return address, just my name in unfamiliar handwriting.

*At the lagoon of Diversey Harbor,
in the cavity of the northmost tree,
reach in and find a pulley,
securing a gift from me.*

I did as the riddle told me. Diversey Harbor was different then—wilder, older somehow. The north end is where an ancient oak twists from cracked concrete, its roots breaking through like gnarled toes. As the letter said, the owl hole was there, a perfect dark cavity in the tallest tree. The park felt damp and alive, crawling with ancient bugs and decaying ivy. Reaching inside, I found the rusted chain of a lengthy pulley, where a safe lowered from the tippy top down to my hands. There, another oracle was attached.

> *In this safe, a fortune so grand*
> *A hundred twenty thousand, in your hand*
> *The key to the lock will be revealed in plain sight*
> *But only if you wait til the timing is right.*

I shook the box, a light clamor. Scared, I looked over my shoulder. What if someone was out to get me? It was a beautiful fall day by the lake. As far as I could tell, there was no one to fear. I put the safe in my backpack and wrapped it before me, protecting it with my life. I made my way south toward home. I did again what the letter said: Trusted and waited.

> *A beat.*

When my mother died, she left me all the money she had. I'd been lucky to receive it. Made a down payment on my first home. At that point, I had a good job. But after losing her, I kept looking for signs everywhere. In coffee grounds, in cloud patterns, in the way stage lights caught dust in the air. Maybe that's why the oracle found me.

The money didn't feel like mine because nothing felt real without her. I couldn't help but feel. . . the money wasn't for me.

I endured an icy winter, then finally, one day in early spring:

Something unfamiliar appeared like a mirage on a familiar block I passed every day. In a formerly boarded-up building, a burning violet sign said CLAIRVOYANT, an unexpected solar blast exploding from years of sludge and soot. Inside, the fluorescent lights buzzed and flickered, animating metal racks lined with keys—hundreds of them, maybe thousands, twitching in the shadows. The woman at the desk didn't look up, but something about her stillness felt deliberate—like she'd been waiting.

She appeared to be no clairvoyant at all, just some haggard midwestern woman hunched over a desk in a messy, fluorescent shop. Tinkering with a padlock. She didn't even look at me. *Can I help you?* she asks.

I say *I don't think so. I'm sorry.* Defeated, I turn to leave. *Are you Daniel?* I freeze. *Who wants to know?*

She gets up from her spinning stool, creaks to a wall of labeled keyrings, and says, *Someone left a key for you. I don't know where it leads.* I can't see her eyes. A big hood casts a shadow over them.

I ran my way home, breathless, and finally opened the safe. Another key? I was furious! Was this some kind of a joke? Then it occurred to me. . . It was a copy of my key to this very room in the parochial school.

A beat.

Now that we're inside, I think you should check your pockets. What if there's a final oracle?

COREY and MAXINE reach into their pockets. The Christmas lights sway slightly in the strained flow of air. MAXINE finds a note on folded yellow pad paper. Her hands tremble as she unfolds it. Her voice wavers slightly as she reads:

MAXINE
*Two halves of the sum are tucked away
at the bottom of the box where candies lay
The stash stays secret, no one to know
until two right hands come to show.*

MAXINE and COREY bolt to the vending machine, tripping over one another. They kneel at the receiving door and look at one another.

COREY
Are you ready?

MAXINE
Are you?

They reach in their right hand in unison and pull out two checks. Sixty thousand dollars apiece.

COREY
Daniel!

*DANIEL claps and cheers. He takes a dramatic bow.
MAXINE cocks her head to the side.*

DANIEL
Don't worry. These are just prop checks. Starting this
Friday, real money will be deposited biweekly into your
bank account.

DANIEL and COREY laugh. MAXINE looks distraught.

MAXINE
When did you put the note in my pocket?

DANIEL
Me? I didn't touch your pocket. You'd have to consult a
cleric.

MAXINE
No, seriously. Where did this all come from?

DANIEL
Who's to say? Therein lies the enigma of the oracle.

MAXINE
Come on. Can't you tell me what this is? What was the
inspiration?

DANIEL
Oh, don't spoil the magic, Maxine. It'll ruin all the fun.

He takes a beat. MAXINE looks at the floor.

I want this to be a memorable year for you both—productive, fruitful, and, most importantly, imaginative. Challenge each other. Reflect on each other. Your differences and similarities: the mentor and the protégé, fated by forces we could never even imagine, let alone conjure. Separate but one, like two koi in a pond.

ACT II: SCENE IV

Maxine couldn't stop talking about Daniel's story. She paced our apartment, agitated about how he presented it as truth before revealing it as performance. I told her the oracle was a common theatre trope, watching her reject this simple explanation with increasing desperation.

She insisted that I couldn't possibly understand her concern. She described eerie synchronicities emerging from the private realm to the public through clenched teeth. Little did she know I understood perfectly, not because of synchronicities but because I recognized evidence of my own metaphysical meddling leaking into the third dimension.

She wobbled while walking, perturbed and off-balance. It was a joy for me to see how the mystical fueled her continuing manic behavior. The oracle had triggered something, hopefully a fixture of one of her nightmares.

I loved watching her lose control. She grew overly suspicious, wondering aloud during our entire walk home why the story felt so spiritual. She wanted to share more but thought it wouldn't be safe. The forces of the oracle could be untrustworthy, she said.

Once we were in, I stood in the glory of the window, processing it all. From the street, I imagined I looked like a queen, overseeing the chaos of my design. I fixated on a flickering streetlamp, tapping my foot in excitement.

I ran over the details in my mind, fact-checking backward then forward. Supernatural occurrences were commonplace in dramatic writing, as were oracles. Clairvoyants existed outside of my realm. Inexplicable mysteries weren't unique to me. Violet was a regular color of neon. But I couldn't shake the evidence. Daniel's inspiration had come through some secret tunnel from me.

I'd underestimated him. I didn't feel steady. The man was a bumbling fool over text, and now I knew he was a magician. What if he intentionally hid some calculating part of himself? The possibility made me wet. Was he a performer, and was it all good fun? Or was he a good man with a dark secret? I prayed for the latter. With the latter, it was the start of an incomparable affair.

I ran my tongue along the inside of my cheek at the thought of it. I really liked him. I needed to stop it. I needed control. There was no time to be so genuinely enticed by a man. He was a distraction. I needed to focus on my work first and monitor Maxine second. She shuffled about, insufferably humming anxious tunes, casting objects around the room, in a panic, without a vision.

She wasn't wrong that there were signs in everything —I'd made sure of it. Every reminder that her life was a story turned to doom thrilled me more. She was even wearing house slippers like the ones I'd been given in the den. *Don't stop, don't stop. It feels so good.*

MAXINE
Stop!

She was screaming at the train. We lived beside the elevated tracks of the brown line. The apartment shook whenever the train passed. I wished they'd keep going into her, shaking her to her death. Every time one passed, I crossed my fingers, trying to pass the chaos straight into her soul.

To tune it out, she decided to put on a record player. The soft, staticky spin of vinyl, then the thump of the needle. *Thunk.* A piano. Whatever it was, it didn't have the effect on her that she wanted. Her body clenched. She stomped into the kitchen, unhinged. A downstairs neighbor pounded at the ceiling. She stomped back.

I was thankful for the neighbors' interference. Right on cue, I wanted to see how far I could push it with Maxine, who was increasingly paranoid. I wanted to create just enough of a scene to test it.

I dragged a dusty bottle of cabernet straight from my luggage and took Maxine's magnetic corkscrew from the fridge. A glass of wine might steady her nerves or, better yet, fray them further.

I jammed the opener into the cork, straight through the foil, watching her from the corner of my eye. On pins and needles, Maxine swarmed over and snatched the bottle, exactly as I hoped she would.

COREY
Can't you relax?

MAXINE

How can I when you're opening this in the most
irreverent way? This isn't a college party.

COREY

You think it's immature? You're dragging around
furniture late at night and stomping like *Fee-fi-fo-fum*!

*COREY jumps up and down so hard that the neighbor
starts banging again.*

MAXINE

Don't be a brat.

COREY

Am I a brat, or are your panties in a wad?

MAXINE

They are! Don't you see how worried I am? Answer me.
Who are they? What if they're all a part of it? The source
of my nightmares, whoever is trying to get Daniel, and the
banging neighbors.

COREY

Oh, come on.

MAXINE

It's the truth. You're not paying attention.

COREY

Maxine. The oracle isn't real. It's a made-up, fanciful tale.

MAXINE

You're not listening to me.

COREY

I am. I'm worried about you.

MAXINE

Because you don't understand the context, I thought
maybe you'd finessed your interpretive skills on top of
growing up and stabbing me in the back. But here you are,
with the answers right before you, and you're still acting
like an illiterate amateur. Use critical thinking. See the
evidence. Have the thought.

COREY

You're not making any sense. There is no evidence! There
is nothing to have proof of. You're sleep-deprived, having
bad dreams, and finding too many coincidences. You need
sleep! I apologize for what I did, but don't let it set the
tone. I am not, nor is anyone else, out to get you.

MAXINE

I told you I'm not feeling well, so why are you yelling at
me? You should be trying to calm me down.

COREY

You're making me mad. It's not fair for you to expect me
to interpret things just as you do. I'm not you, so don't
treat me like some dollar-store hand mirror!

MAXINE

You think I want to pitch a fit like this? I hate all these
exclamation marks! I hate that you throw them back,

imitating me! All you're doing is reflecting me! If you're not a hand mirror, stop yammering in my face!

It was perfect. She delivered the Tony-winning agitation I hoped would send the altercation to the next tier. We officially caused a commotion. With that, I stomped one final time into the ground as hard as possible, ensuring the *boom* would echo through the joints of the building.

Silence.

Then, the sound of a door flying open. An angry grunt. Rapid footsteps came up the stairs. Bang, bang, bang. Pounding on the door. Bang, bang, bang.

MAXINE
Why would you do that? We could be in danger.

COREY
It's my fault. Let me throw on a sweater. I'll talk to them.

I slipped into my room, put fifty dollars and an oracle into an envelope, and reemerged in a sweatshirt. As I vanished out the front door, I saw Maxine putting her head in her hands and leaning on the kitchen counter.

Everything was going exactly according to plan.

A long pause. Faded mumbling and murmuring outside. MAXINE backs across the room up on the wall, staring at the closed door. After a while, COREY reenters sheepishly.

A long pause. Faded mumbling and murmuring outside.

MAXINE backs across the room and leans her back against the wall, staring at the closed door. After a long beat, COREY reenters sheepishly.

MAXINE
Well?

COREY
They're mad.

MAXINE
No shit. And?

COREY
I promise it won't happen again.

MAXINE
Here is the recurring issue, Corey. You get me twisted in the head. I hated you all summer, then dreaded seeing you today. And it's just. I want to have fun with you and move past what you did. But you continue to get under my skin on purpose. *Nag, nag, nag.* I wish you would listen to me instead of picking a fight. Then I could trust you and talk through some of these things. We have potential. Don't insist on spoiling it.

I had to stop myself from smiling. She was setting herself up perfectly. She needed something from me, something only I could give her. An inescapable force laded our potential, but she didn't need to know that.

COREY
I do have fun with you. And you're right. I don't want to

nag. I don't want to make fun of each other. I'd never forgive myself if we spent the year at each other's throats. We should be something special, not a missed opportunity.

MAXINE

I won't make fun of you anymore. I'm sorry that I did.

Then, I planted a new seed. A glimmer of hope that I was on her side against whoever was *a part of it*, whatever it was to her. In a way, Professor Due taught me how to manage the situation and live in the moment. She always gave good lessons. For her to trust me, I'd have to show I was genuinely on her side, whether it was truly genuine or not.

COREY

I admit it. I had a weird feeling about his story, too. Please don't judge me.

MAXINE

I would never judge you. See? This is what I mean. If we're in it together, maybe we can solve it and restore the displaced energy.

COREY

You're right that it felt sinister. I want to like Daniel, and I do. I don't think it's his fault. I'm scared something is after us, you and me. Maybe it used Daniel as a medium. Whatever it is, we can work together to clear it up. We can light candles, incense, and put on trash television. Whatever the modern ritual is. We can get deep or have fun hanging out. I'm here for you, no matter what.

MAXINE gives COREY a big, big hug.

MAXINE

Thank you. I love you. We can do all the above. Thank you for not judging me. I'm getting aggressive, and I can feel myself doing it. I really should get some sleep.

Maxine kissed me on my hairline and gave me one more squeeze. She shook her head and laughed, probably at how we escalated and then landed with relief. She said goodnight, entered her bedroom, and closed the door. The piano music ended, and the vinyl spun—*thump, crackle, crackle, thump.*

Instructions for an excellent magic trick:

STEP ONE: If you find yourself with a mentor losing her grip on reality, mirror her paranoia until she's irate. Once she's enraged, she attracts outside attention by making a scene.
STEP TWO: When neighbors come pounding, speak to them privately. Tell them it's a prank and that you're sorry.
STEP THREE: Slip your neighbors a fifty-dollar bill, a pack of moving tape, and an oracle. [Ask them to rewrite it if your opponent knows your handwriting.]
STEP FOUR: Ask them to return, take the stairs, and tape the oracle to your opponent's bedroom window.
STEP FIVE: Then, return quietly, settle down, and plant an unsettling idea. Tell your opponent goodnight, let her go into her bedroom, be patient, and wait. Soon, you will hear her start screaming.

ACT II: SCENE V

COREY and MAXINE's apartment.

The trick worked. My oracle kicked Maxine from mania into desolation.

The creature escaping from your dream
slithers to the lake through a sewer stream
And soon, the riptide drags you near
an ancient curse that feeds on fear

Days and hours passed. By early October, her physical presentation deteriorated by the minute.

As September moved along, her clothing transmogrified into chronic wrinkles, her silhouette went lumpy, and the natural imperfections of linen, which added character, transformed into unignorable blemishes.

She became hideous. I couldn't look away.

Picking Maxine to pieces became a grotesque fascination. An addiction. No different, psychologically, than a porn compulsion. In the same way as porn, Maxine's demeanor mimicked reality but was inherently off-balance. Wrong. Unnatural.

After I stole Daniel's idea, my crush grew bigger. The fear he instilled in me got me hot. By the time I started fantasizing about him in my private pleasures, my thrills were accelerated, with Maxine as the point of comparison. She was that, and I was this, and oh my god, I was so bad.

Even during the first week, she overflowed the kitchen sink. We didn't have a dishwasher, so she clogged the drain, filled the basin with water to soak, meandered off, and forgot it like she had amnesia. I gently knocked on the bathroom door to remind her. With no answer but a groan, I cracked the door open and found her all twisted.

She adopted the posture of a winding snake. She sat for eons like that, perched on the lid of a closed toilet, pretzeled inside the tub, contorted over the sink. Her electric toothbrush had no battery. I don't know how often she said she'd run out for AAs and never did. I didn't hear her toothbrush run once.

Meanwhile, from the ever-flowing sink, scum of left-over dinner cascaded over the edges, running like rivers down the uneven floors. Pieces of Hamburger Helper and scrambled eggs settled into the hollows like stones in a rapid.

Without announcing it, I switched to a diet of raw foods to see what would happen. I ate fresh vegetables, fruit, cheese, and deli meat off a paper plate with a plastic fork. I drank LaCroix, wary of the germs in our sink, and took my trash out in a single grocery sack.

Meanwhile, she wrestled with boxes of macaroni and ramen. When I finally got to them, the labels were tattered and gnawed at, and dry noodles and cheese powder were scattered across the counter. She must've forgotten how to tear a perforation somewhere along the way.

Still, she held onto hope that it was all transitory. She still never mentioned the oracle.

MAXINE

Maybe the move was more disorienting than I thought.
Lack of good sleep is corrupting my function.
Perhaps I'm sensitive to the hormones of early
menopause.

The list went on and, at first, pointed in every direction but at me. She visited a primary care doctor for a physical and ran labs to check her fatigue. Urine and blood. Everything was clear. Pap smear. Mammogram. Nothing amiss.

Doctors affirmed that menopause can be tricky to navigate. She pointed out that she still had her period, and the doctors corrected the diagnosis: perimenopause. She quit smoking, quit drinking, and swapped espresso for green tea.

Amidst all the visits, she started a new diet.

Twelve hundred milligrams of calcium a day. Dark leaves. Sardines. Turmeric. Chilis for her thyroid. Olives and avocados for her heart. Grains for her willpower. Grape-nuts for her anxious gut. Broth to warm goosebumps. Ice to cool sweat.

She ate her weight in grams of protein, but her weight continued to drop. Emaciated. Frantically setting timers to remember to eat, where she'd force-feed herself all these regimented nutrients.

I supported her, just as she asked. I synchronized our schedules wherever possible when it wouldn't detract from my writing. During writing workshops, I kept her involved and enthusiastic throughout the day, and sometimes, we'd travel home together.

At home, I kept practicing my magic tricks, inspired by Daniel and my success with the first one. I was a breakthrough talent!

First, I tried a few lighter ones to lift the mood, ones with mischievous innocence. You know, to help humanize the situation.

COREY hangs a calendar dated a year ahead.
COREY and MAXINE laugh.

COREY swaps MAXINE'S lingerie with swimsuits.
COREY and MAXINE laugh.

COREY puts Play-Doh in the bath drain.
COREY and MAXINE laugh.

MAXINE
Believe it or not, it feels good to make fun of myself. It really helps.

Watching Maxine deteriorate, my fascination with Daniel only intensified. He'd proven himself more than just some guy. He was a true magician, someone who understood the power of illusion. When we worked together, I fantasized about his calloused hands and all the tricks they'd performed.

My attraction to him complicated things. It made being in the workshop room hard, but it was easy to be present when he wasn't around. I wonder what Daniel would think if he knew all my work behind the scenes at home. What would his critique be? Would he be impressed by my skill and dedication to the craft? Or would he recoil?

I fantasized that he was on my side, putting me in a better position to slowly reveal my truth to him. Letting him uncover my tarry insides. But Maxine remained the priority. I couldn't let my feelings for Daniel distract me from the medal I deserved for dismantling her. When Maxine laughed at my pranks, I pictured Daniel in the shadows, applauding my technique. My new, unsuspecting mentor in the art of deception.

Each successful prank confirmed my growing power over her sanity and the fabric of her perception. She trusted my playfulness in a way that almost made me bashful. I felt like a schoolgirl performing tricks for her mom. She had no idea that my innocent tricks were rehearsals for bigger projects.

At the end of week three, I decided to test how far her trust would stretch. We kept a stack of logic puzzles in the bathroom. Spooky mysteries, all in good fun. In each, a description of a mystery to solve, usually a crime, as well as victims, suspects, and perpetrators. The perfect next act in my performance. I selected one from the easy section: strange occurrences, cryptic messages, *Clue*-like slapstick scenarios. Oh my.

I filled in the puzzle halfway with goofy, nonsense answers. My written solutions gave clues that pointed to the victim as the culprit and the culprit as the victim. Even without the clues, the culprit was so obviously the watchman. He lurked around, totally sketchy, right there in plain sight. Maxine stood in my doorway, crying.

MAXINE

This is an easy puzzle. I can't figure this out for my life.
You've done half of it already, and I still can't figure it out.
It's saying the watchman didn't do it, but I see the facts
right there. I must be wrong. I'm always wrong now.

Maxine crumpled to her knees, sobbing over the half-finished puzzle. She pressed her palms against her temples. She was so convinced she was wrong she wasn't willing to consider that she was right. Her self-esteem had all but deteriorated, and she took anything I said as truth.

I knelt beside her.

COREY

Maybe you're overthinking it.

MAXINE grabs and clings onto COREY's elbow.

MAXINE

I need to figure out what's wrong with me. I think I'm
really sick.

I squeezed her hand, savoring the irony as the architect of her undoing. But I couldn't reveal that—Daniel was shaping into a malevolent force in her mind due to the oracle. I needed to keep the focus over there and let her trust me completely.

She attributed my cruelty to good nature, a scrappy little master of funny pranks. I was the helpful class clown. She was preoccupied with understanding why everything was wrong with her, blind to whatever was wrong with me. Had I revealed myself after the logic puzzle of the curse, she may never have trusted me again.

I wouldn't dare. As for the oracle, she'd been the one to call Daniel's a fictitious prophecy. How could she go back on her word after that?

But as for the logic puzzle, she'd had enough and added her name to a waitlist to see a neurologist. Appointments for the neurologist were months out, so I offered to accompany her to a psychiatrist. After a long workshop day, we booked an evening appointment with the first person available.

The psychiatrist's office was in a creepy old bank in Uptown, one of the early Art Deco monuments to commerce gone to seed. It was nearly dark when we arrived, the marble floors reflecting our footsteps in eerie echoes. We found the security man in the building's entry asleep on his desk, head thrown back, mouth agape like a corpse. The elevator was broken, but of course, so we took the stairs, breaking in between twelve flights for Maxine to catch her breath. Each landing is a gaudy new installation shoddily preserved with gold film over the years.

Separate from the stylized geometry of the Art Deco main halls, the psychiatrist's office evoked a nineties dentist's office with full walls of frosted-glass cubes and dark purple carpets. The psychiatrist, an expressionless fellow in his early seventies, barely looked up from his notepad as Maxine described her symptoms. I watched his pen move mechanically across the page, wondering if he was writing anything. He smelled like Red Bull and English Leather and had a mustache that, for sure, smelled even more like Red Bull and English Leather.

Within ten minutes, he'd suggested a late-onset eating disorder, bipolar or a related manic-depressive disorder, and early-onset dementia. He shared the diagnoses like a judge gravely delivering a death sentence. He prescribed her three pills, but Maxine didn't care about all of that. She just wanted something to sleep. The way she clutched the prescriptions reminded me of a helpless cat. Her only hope.

But the guy didn't take insurance and charged two hundred and fifty dollars to prey on her vulnerability. I offered to pitch in, knowing fully well she'd refuse. She was very much aware that she was a burden to all.

From there, we picked up Valium from an all-night pharmacy where fluorescent lights buzzed like angry robots. And it helped. Oh, how it helped. Once she took it, only a half-hour or so before she vanished and zonked. Even a few extra minutes and she'd peter off into delirium, her words slurring out the seams of a chemical straitjacket. Valium was proposed as an answer but kicked off the start of a never-ending medication fiasco.

MAXINE

I've dealt with depression, but this is a new beast. It's like I entered another realm.

ACT II: SCENE VI

The parochial school.

With a dull, screeching nub of chalk, Daniel wrote GET THE SCARY OUT in all caps across the top of a blackboard and underlined it. He turned to us expectantly, raising his eyebrows and pursing his lips.

Once you've been in enough theatre classes, you can accurately detect which exercises are derivatives of WRITE WHAT SCARES YOU. Some artistic leaders felt jazzed enough to create their spinoff, as Daniel did here.

The blackboard still hinted at erased ghost words, ciphers of the past. Touching them left fine dust on my fingertips. If you got chalk on you, it stayed there. Everything felt slightly sticky from improper ventilation. The chair backs, the doorknobs, and even the papers we brought down would curl at the edges after an hour.

On top of that, the uneven heating made cold spots

drift through the room like invisible puddles. Chilly autumns were new to me. The heater was useless, wheezing steam that smelled like rust. I dragged my metal folding chair to where I would sit, its worn-down feet scraping their way along. Maxine looked wired. I didn't want to stare because seeing her hurt me, but I stole glances when I could. She wore pale, wrinkled Levi's—one ankle rolled up and the other left down—and a stained school spirit shirt from our college. It was too cold to be out without a jacket, yet there she was. No makeup, hair undone, and glasses.

I had never seen her in regular glasses, only the novelty-looking reading ones she'd bring to class occasionally. Sometimes, she'd put the glasses on while reading our work, smiling indulgently, massaging her hands with the utmost pleasure of being our teacher. In college, she treated our writing like snacks and read it as if it were the yummiest, most unique thing she'd ever encountered.

That day, her interest in art mirrored that of an under-slept college student—the ripening of years of practice out the window, replaced by the frenzied rush of an artist coming of age. The fervor fascinated me. Her demented aura added interest. She was an art piece of her own, reverting from the uptightness that naturally came with growing into a deranged, risk-taking pursuit. God help her. She was in a world of trouble if her coming of age was anything like that.

Daniel's take on WRITE WHAT SCARES YOU, as he described, wasn't about *recognizing* what scares us but discovering ways to discuss our fears with other collaborators. He argued that we could get to the root of the fear more easily through conversation. From there, we could find ways to write it into our plays. He slammed the original WRITE WHAT SCARES YOU because, to him, it implied isolation in fear. He was saddened by the thought of someone recording their deepest horrors onto paper, never to be seen unless the work was published. I agreed with him on that. If our secrets never saw daylight, how would we know we were revealing too much before it was too late?

I smiled darkly to myself. I knew I was entirely missing the point.

He held up a red egg timer, set it for twenty-five minutes, and placed it between Maxine and me. Off we went into the vast but private landscapes of our internal worlds. The ticking underscored the frantic dotting and crossing of our pens on paper. I felt like Maxine's and my words were competing in a close race as if the winner would be the woman who wrote the most words. As if there would be a winner at all.

It was impossible to make the hand move as fast as the mind. The pace of the hand had to be trained. I always mourned the many ideas lost from brain to paper, but it was hopeless. As people, we were naturally restricted. Had we been spirits, the words would have escaped us without a problem.

Even psychologically defunct, Maxine was an artist with far more training. Thus, as I looked over at the scribbling in her thin, classic, emerald-green pen, I despaired at the rapidly increasing length of her paragraphs. I started to tremble, feeling time extend like it was spaghettifying in a black hole. Every second that passed made the noodles thinner.

It wasn't the prompt's fault. On the contrary, WRITE WHAT SCARES YOU probed a verbose manifesto about the fears of losing my powers. But I couldn't put that down, so instead I dallied on about being shy. The slow, patient cursive of my first few sentences degraded into the erratic etchings of a serial killer. I didn't care what I wrote, but I needed to learn to write faster than she did.

The timer beeped suddenly and loudly, and we both jumped and gasped.

Maxine wrote two pages, and I only wrote one. I hated losing to her.

That said, I felt sure that her competition with me was the last thing on her mind. We were instructed to write about fear, and I eagerly anticipated whatever sick fascination I would develop with whatever she shared. I couldn't wait to see what was scaring her after our tumultuous, solutionless battle with her mental health throughout September.

DANIEL

Maxine, you may go first. No need to read verbatim. Tell us what your process was like. What fears came to you?

MAXINE shakes out her hand. She shuffles the paper in order.

MAXINE

All this last month, I spent what feels like all my free time trying to diagnose whatever it is that's making me sick. I didn't get any answers.

Beat.

Trying to pursue an answer, I lost trust in my instincts. I feel done with that now. After all my efforts, it's clear that this isn't a spiral of my own but interference from the otherworldly. My fear was admitting that to myself and, congruently, admitting it to the two of you.

Beat.

You may be concerned, but you must understand that I've arrived at something. You know what I mean, Daniel. It's hard to trust you if you don't fess up. Tell me more about your oracle.

Her voice intensified the longer she talked—bolded, italicized, and highlighted with freaked-out hysteria. A thing to be awed. I slid down my chair, afraid she might lash out like one of those gorillas going viral. That's how little of a human she seemed.

Outside, a goblin shrub screeched its nail against the screen. But as much as I wanted to retreat in fear, I couldn't stop searching for Maxine. I searched for her there as thoroughly as I could. The idea that she could be empowered by rebellious self-resolve was catastrophic for me.

If she started illuminating the truth, I'd have to shift my strategy again.

If that were the case, this round of my involvement with the curse would be trickier. I'd no longer be managing Maxine's behavior if she decided to go rogue. I would have to dictate everyone else's perception of her somehow. At the mention of the oracle, Daniel turned his head to the side. He sat on his hands. His energy dimmed in a rift of confusion. He asked for clarification.

DANIEL
My oracle? The story I performed at welcome night.

MAXINE transfigures from vulnerable into defensive.

MAXINE
See? This is exactly why I hesitate to share. You pretend it
wasn't real.

Maxine pulled the tattered yellow pad sheet from her
back pocket. She stood and presented it to us separately as
though it were a sacred artifact to be respected and
feared. There it was: the proof of her oracle. It had been
posted in the night outside of her bedroom window. The
paper trembled in her grip, making rapid, nervous
patterns like hard rain on a tin roof. Then, *presto!* She
popped it open like a scroll in Daniel's face.

Daniel reached slowly in front of him, his neck still
twisted sideways and took the paper. He wrinkled his
brows and inspected it. He read it repeatedly, holding it at
different angles as if it would help him make sense of it.

DANIEL
Maxine, I'm a little confused. Are you joking with me?
Did you do this during the exercise?

MAXINE
See what I mean? Don't do that. I knew you would do
that. I can't trust you!

DANIEL

Okay. Okay, okay. We're fine. I'm just asking. Corey, did
you write this?

COREY

No.

DANIEL

Guys, come on. Is this a prank? You got me. I want to do
the fear exercise.

MAXINE

This *is* the exercise! Daniel, you know my handwriting.

Maxine held up evidence of her handwriting, and I
held up evidence of mine. I clarified that it got crazy at
the bottom of the page because I ran out of time. My
pulse rose. I wouldn't allow Maxine's oracle to trace back
to me. What followed was a painful descent into Maxine's
paranoia.

MAXINE

How am I meant to believe that it just so *happens* on the
very week I move to Chicago, after many months of
nightmares, specifically that a sea creature crawled from
the underworld, escaped the prisonous confines of my
skull, and slithered off into Lake Michigan, that *this* is a
made-up coincidental piece of nothing?

She smacks a fist on the oracle note.

What do you want? To prove that I'm ill? I'm not. This is
happening. We must face it. I'm living proof of

interference. An evil realm is manipulating me. The same sinister force that possessed you to write this.

DANIEL

Maxine, I promise you. There's no real coincidence, as far as I'm concerned. Otherworldly messages are a great trope of theatre. You taught me that. You are having anxiety, and as a friend, I'm here to support you through it. Maybe we should get you help.

MAXINE

You can't make me believe these overlaps are natural. You're gaslighting me, but I won't let you anymore. Never mind what I wrote. I will tell you about my dream.

Beat.

A snake in the toilet grows into a sea monster. Somewhere between flushes, drains, and sewers, the sickness gives it new powers. It grows into a beast to be feared, half lady, half serpent.

The beast stays distant at first, swimming off in the buoys. But she comes closer to shore, ungracefully and without shame. Her body writhes along the sand.

She stinks like the worst of Chicago's waste. A breeze travels across from the Indiana Dunes and propels her stench toward me, gusts of cigarette butts and repugnant excrements.

Her hair is knotted and sopping, matted to her head with

animal waste. I watch, intrigued, wanting to run but savoring the image.

The cold distracts me from the monster. In the dream, I grow homesick for Texas, a place of temporary transience. I feel nostalgic for those warm summers, the feelings akin to those restful pauses that come every year in Chicago with the arrival of snow. In the dream, I know I've lost connection with my home city, seeing firsthand how it transformed into a place of horror in my absence.

The despair leaves me inspired and wild, but my subconscious knows it's sick.

I walk in. Shards of hail started falling out of the sky again, making the horizon of water and outer space nearly indistinguishable. Ice touching down and melting around me, losing itself in my warmth. I get further into the raging pool, an ice bath up to my knees.

I was stunned and moved by each detail of this story but viscerally troubled. Mentally, I was transported to a dark theatre, an unnamed Greek tragedy. I wanted to protect the characters and save them, knowing they were inching toward doom because the chorus had revealed the ending in the beginning but was still selfishly dying to witness that doom happen.

Maxine paused for breath throughout her telling, creating dark, empty fields of space for me to retreat into my private reactions, swelling with feeling and staring at the stars. Hearing her plight, I was everywhere at once. I was in the tragic audience, under the big Texas skies, in Mélusine's magic time mirror, and there, in that parochial basement, all at once. I felt both inside myself and beside myself. She continued.

MAXINE

The beast widened her mouth, her jaw unhinged, and the stench nearly knocked me out. Her fangs were sharp but halfway rotted, mossy with the plaque of urban trash. Her hands were so small that she wore aluminum pop tops as rings, ripping the surrounding skin apart.

Her bra was constructed of newspapers, matted to her breasts with dog piss. Her belly button was a well of scabs that she'd picked and re-picked, flaky with infection. Then, I wake up with these.

Maxine lowered her shaking hands to her ankles and lifted the bottoms of her pant legs to her knees. At first, it looked like a mirage, but slowly, the ambiguous shape materialized—two muddy handprints wrapped around her calves.

MAXINE

As the serpent rose above me, I ran. I sprinted to the shoreline as fast as possible but didn't make it. I screamed, and no one came for me. The beach was sparse on such a cold day. This woman, this loathsome creature, grabbed me and dragged me, desperate to pull me down.

Maxine sounded so sincere it was disorienting. I wanted to indulge in her fantasy, the dissonance growing inside me. She remained stoic and sure, unwavering. The markings on her calves were grotesque but all wrong. Did her fear of the oracle drive her to self-harm? I feared her mental state more than I feared the serpent. What if her ideas held the potential to lead to truth, to lead to me?

COREY
Show me again.

MAXINE lifts the pants faster this time.

I got on the ground before her as delicately as I would if I were praying to her at an altar. I inspected the hand-prints. They weren't quite human, but there was something definitively feminine about the fingers. They looked long and sure, like they hadn't trembled while grabbing.

There were abstract pricks at the edge of each line where the fingertips would be. Ten scabby pricks from ten sharp nails. Maxine said the dreams started in Dallas, convinced they'd burrowed in their early forms and followed her through the infrastructure between side-walks, up the walls, and into our floorboards. She glared at me as I sat down at her feet.

COREY
Why are you looking at me like that? I'm trying to help.

MAXINE
By gawking in disgust?

She'd gotten gruff. I needed to calm her down. I placed my hands as gently as I could on her injuries and rubbed them. Daniel stood by, unsure of what to do. I mended the wounds as meaningfully as possible, trying to channel the platonic but intimate care I'd promised that night in Dallas before her word was broken.

Her legs seemed to crumble in my hands. I felt her get weaker with the touch of my mouth, and she started to cry. She wiped her snotty nose on a loose sheet of notebook paper and sat up to face me. Her lower lip trembled, purple and numb-looking.

MAXINE

I haven't visited the worst of it. She told me you had sent her.

I got vertigo. I pulled my knees to my chest and shifted away from her, my limbs pulsating in horror.

COREY

Stop that. What do you want me to say to that?

DANIEL looks at COREY, bewildered.

DANIEL

Hey, hey. Let's settle down now. Maxine, that was a scary but beautiful dream. Thank you for sharing with us. If it's okay, I'd like to revisit the wounds on your legs later. I'm worried about you, so I will follow up.

Beat.

While I can appreciate you committing to the character, and I do, I don't know if getting Corey wrapped up in theatrics is the best thing here. She's getting excited, and I want this to be a safe, level space for all.

MAXINE

Then how do you explain the overlaps?

DANIEL

I chalk it up to coincidences. As we've long pointed out, similar similarities show up in human literature worldwide. Maxine, maybe this will help. Corey's proposal for the residency is about an otherworldly sea creature, too. One of a different sort, in France. I've also referenced this sort of beast in my works.

COREY

Yes! Daniel's right. There are many mermaid stories. It's not a reflection of us conspiring against you. It's a mythical framework that many people enjoy! The reality is there's nothing sinister happening. Maybe it's simpler. Maybe it's that we're all just a cliché.

DANIEL

That's a perfect point. See? There are parallels between your two projects, too.

MAXINE

You two are depraved. These aren't fun little creatures. They're wicked entities, not to be provoked.

DANIEL

There are unusual overlaps. I'll give you that. But I'm disturbed by this. I need you to understand I made the story up. I'm a professional magician. It's part of why we're friends. I'd never intend to hurt you.

Beat.

As for right now, I'm very sorry. This exercise was meant to alleviate fear, not aggravate it. I don't know where this note came from. I suspect you wrote it when you were over-exhausted and forgot. That is a hypothesis, but none of this is your fault.

Daniel suggested it might be helpful to disclose the methods of his trick. His description had no magic, only opportune moments to place props discreetly. The vending machine moment was luck. When I went to get the Pixy Stix before Maxine arrived, he tensed up. I missed them. He attributed it to the fact that I didn't miss anything. I just wasn't looking for anything.

Maxine continued rolling her eyes and shaking her head, disgusted by him. She started raising her voice angrily, insinuating Daniel was vomitous for continuing to lie to her face even when confronted. She said it was, without comparison, the nastiest and most scornful thing a man could do to a woman. She said she would spit in his face if we weren't on the theatre campus.

Daniel didn't look hurt, only increasingly concerned. He remained calm, breathing deeply, allowing her hot-wired misconceptions to cool. His plan wasn't working. His alleged gaslighting ignited the increasing disquiet of a woman's wrath. He should've thought harder before he started mouthing his defense. The man didn't recognize that once a woman reached that state, he was stuck on the battle's losing side. Advocating for himself added kerosene to the fire. That was mistake number one.

Daniel's second mistake was explaining the magic trick. When someone adds too many details to their alibi, it becomes more of a lie. Had he not watched any crime documentaries? Had he never been caught in a lie before? These were skills he should have built over time. That is my critique of him.

Maxine's eyes went black in her fury. Her voice became a thunder of battering, unrestrained, ferocious disparagement directed at Daniel, who remained astonished.

She paced around the room, pointing out every coincidence, every overlap, building evidence of some grand supernatural conspiracy. It was all connected, but she couldn't yet see how. All she knew for sure was that the clues led to a menacing nautical prophecy, that it was all connected in some horrible grid. Daniel was one of, if not *the*, masterminds behind it.

As for my involvement, she couldn't prove it for sure, but she was onto me. That I better start confessing, or she'd hand me my ass. At the very least, she said, I was some spineless, eldritch operative. Waxing poetic about me being the stereotypical nurse, reinforcing her hysteria with my many acts of medical support. She was exactly right. Spot-on. I'd be more concerned if she didn't mention all the coincidences like a deranged maniac.

My brain was muddy. I couldn't think. I had to step away. I pried myself free from our thorny emotional entanglement and tiptoed to the bathroom door, afraid she may jump out at me or grab my legs like a subject in need of an exorcist.

My forearms stayed bumpy in coldness and fear. Crossing the basement, I don't think I breathed once. Then, when I finally made it to the shabby, flickering bathroom, I collapsed on the toilet. My pulse pounded between my eyes. She'd been right. And if she'd known she'd been right, she would have tried to hurt us, I was sure.

Despite my recent ventures into the metaphysical, I was a physical person. Unable to reground without stark, sensory stimulation. I twisted the squeaking, unhinged knob of icy sink water and plunged my face into the basin. A couple of splashes and no luck. I only got colder.

I scoured an overcrowded toiletry cabinet for something else. I grit my teeth, knocking over abandoned body sprays, vintage Tampax boxes, and nude-colored footies. A silverfish scurried away from beneath a single, lost character's shoe.

On top of an ancient coffee-stained workshop draft of Noah Haidle's *Smokefall*, I found my only last hope, a Pond's cold cream container. From what I could tell, Pond's had no expiration date, but if it had, this particular box would have gone rancid in the early nineties. I smeared it everywhere I could and waited for the anxiety to cool.

I pressed my head to the door and breathed heavily, bracing myself for what to do next. I couldn't do anything myself at that point. I needed to keep Daniel in the role of the red herring. I needed him. He could take the brunt of the blame if only I angled the stage just right. His exercise had backfired spectacularly. He was a convincing enemy. I decided to take her to Daniel.

I emerged and returned, the lethal level of toxicity of the room still intact. We needed to get out.

COREY

I have an idea. Let's take a break! We'll go for a walk and get some fresh, cool air. Better yet, why don't we walk to the lagoon at Diversey Harbor? You can check the owl hole yourself.

DANIEL

That's a really good idea, Corey. I think we all need a

pause. On the way back, we'll regroup. If we decide to come back after, I'll get us some lunch along the way.

Max accepted the challenge with rabid determination. She frantically threw her belongings together, yanking her sweater inside out. She didn't bother to smooth out the static frenzy in her hair. She stuffed her work slides into her backpack and jammed her feet back into her rain boots by the door. It'd rained most of the month.

She huffed in exasperation while Daniel and I moved more tepidly, buttoning our cardigans, checking for our wallets, and trying to reorient. Whatever we might find at the harbor, I knew the day would be a turning point. Whether we turned toward a resolution or further into descent remained to be seen. We got out the door while Maxine berated us for trying to explain it all away.

ACT II: SCENE VII

Diversey Harbor on Lake Michigan.

I linked my elbows with Maxine like usual and headed in that direction. We were a mess, stark against multi-million-dollar walk-ups and red brick condominiums.

Fit blondes in full Nike sweatsuits jogged past with their beautiful children in expensive joggers. Young men still in business wear made their way home from the L station with paper sacks full of Whole Foods. Just a few weeks ago, Maxine would have blended in seamlessly. The last time she lived in Chicago, she probably blended in even more.

Before, she'd been a standout, glimmering with poise, every crease where it should be, always prepared. Now, she walked with a limp, agonizing over an injury she'd painted on herself. By the severe wrinkle in her brow, I believe it did hurt, but maybe not in the way she thought.

The three of us inched along the path toward

Diversey Harbor, squinting against whips of lake spray. Maxine sped-walked onward in an exhausting game of Follow the Leader. A baleful gray had settled over the shore, the wind an unseasonable chill. Her agitation grew with every step, her words flinging in a torrent about signs and symbols we were too arrogant to see.

She jabbed a finger toward two women on the shore singing in French, their voices carrying a folk song in the wind. She screamed at them, demanding to know who they were working for. The women looked at Daniel and me helplessly. I said sorry and that our friend wasn't feeling well. Then, Maxine whirled on me and said I was a traitor, even worse than a man.

We oscillated between reasoning with her and giving her space, but she contorted our every move into further proof of conspiracy. The clouds went black. Daniel mentioned we should hurry before the weather turned. Maxine asked him if he commanded the storms now.

Maxine plowed on in a diehard loop-de-loop her rain boots squealing against the pavement. We were sightseeing evidence of conspiracy: a man with a typewriter in the grass was the Great Oracle Writer. A broken half-bench submerged in a puddle was the Throne of the Unsuspecting. A gaggle of geese comprised of water demons in disguise. They fled the city after she leaned into them and vociferated.

I tried to be an agent for distraction, but she was onto me anyway.

COREY
She can take her time. We brought her here for a reason.
She'll check for the pulley, and then we'll go to the deli.

MAXINE

Do you think I don't see your signals to each other?
Your little looks? The way you finish each other's
sentences?

DANIEL

We're just worried about you, Max.

MAXINE

You're both working for them.

By the time we reached the lagoon, thunder rolled
toward Chicago. In the distance, looking east after many
miles of ocean-like water, shadows of rain were approach-
ing. There was just a little time left.

Maxine rushed ahead of us, thrusting her arm into the
hollow and thrashing about inside it. She nearly disappeared into the socket as she probed deeper, desperate.
Her torso was still inside the tree as she turned to us, eyes
wide.

MAXINE

What did you do with it?

DANIEL raises his hands in surrender.

DANIEL

There was never any chain, Max. It was only a story.
Please, you're going to hurt yourself.

He tried to help her stabilize, but she twisted her arm
and stumbled backward. Her eyes were wild, her hair a
tangling nest, her sweater still inside-out and askew. She

held her arms wide to make her body as big as possible and yowled at the whole city:

MAXINE

You've been corrupted! Evil has spread everywhere. There is no use reasoning, especially with the two of you.

Before either of us could react, she bolted southward toward the sandy beaches. We chased and chased, but she moved with supernatural speed, possessed by her delusions. Daniel and I ran in tandem, but eventually he outpaced me, his adrenaline cued up, dead set on saving her.

Once Maxine arrived at the coastline, she didn't even stop for breath before she jetted off into the water. She crashed into the waves, fully clothed, swimming with powerful strokes toward the depths.

DANIEL sprints to the shore's edge.

DANIEL

Maxine! The riptide! Come back!

He kicked off his shoes and dove after her, into the fierce waves. A lifeguard tower stood empty, too cold now for patrol. I sprinted toward the nearest emergency call box. Maxine soon passed the buoys, thrusting through the water with inhuman force. Her head bobbed recklessly like a child's lost ball, vanishing from the shore.

I kept running, scanning for help, anyone at all. The rest of the people cleared up when the rain started coming. My whole chest thundered. I wanted Maxine gone, but not like this, not while Daniel watched alongside, traumatized, trying to help. This wasn't the ending I wanted. It was all too sudden. I wasn't spiritually prepared.

Daniel's voice carried over the wind. Between gulps and gasping, he told her to keep her head up, to lean back and kick if she had to. But she was beyond hearing, beyond reason.

The emergency speedboat appeared along the charcoal horizon, skidding across unpredictable currents with red, yellow, and blue cop lights strobing in chaos. A rescue officer dove into the black, grabbing her by the arm and dragging her with all his might against the water, which was furiously sucking her in. At that point, she'd been in the water for nearly ten minutes.

An ambulance hurried in and paramedics poured out the back door. Maxine was shaking and frigid but quickly reviving. It was a hell of a road, but she would be okay. With her final scrap of energy, she bellowed at everyone in earshot.

MAXINE

Time tries to terminate history, but it will not succeed!

Everyone heard her but no one listened. She screamed it until she went hoarse.

It didn't matter. By that point, her every utterance sounded crazy. A few EMTs worked on getting her warm and loading her in while another nursed Daniel, who was shivering in shock under an emergency blanket. *Were we the family?* No. *Where was the family?* Overseas. We didn't know where. *What the hell happened?* We didn't know. Maybe a manic episode. *Why were we at the lake?* It was kind of a long story. If we gave too many details, they might think we were lying. I was, but only a little.

ACT II: SCENE VIII

In transit, leaving the lake.

The late October wind died down upon Maxine's rescue.

The lake's erratic waves pulled back and settled as if they'd also tired out during the battle of her life and needed to rest. We all needed rest, even me.

Daniel asked if we should call a cab and follow behind Maxine's ambulance, but we were advised by emergency services to go home and recuperate ourselves. We would get stuck in a waiting room, they said, and could even potentially exacerbate conflicts while they formulated a treatment plan.

Since we weren't related to her, tracking her parents with so few details could prove quite the challenge. Her care plan would be a fog, based on what they could tell. It would be best to keep us off-site.

Daniel pressed for details on what to expect.

A female EMT came over with a clipboard. At the hospital, Maxine needed hands-on physical rehabilitation and, more importantly, a psychological evaluation. There were many missing pieces. As soon as Max underwent an emergency CT scan, her behavior could very well indicate a neurological abnormality, such as a tumor. After that, an on-site psychiatrist would visit her to develop a prognosis.

I said I was Maxine's roommate, and that Max had ventured all over the city for a full month for answers. I described it as a whodunit and was factual with the details. She asked about any potential diagnoses, and I told her what the psychiatrist said—malnourishment from late-onset anorexia, a sensitivity to perimenopause, or bipolar disorder. She scoffed and shook her head as she wrote out the details.

Typical, she murmured—the usual slapped-on labels male doctors put onto women without a holistic picture. She asked where we had visited, and I told her about the old bank. She threw the pen down, which swung, tied by a fraying shoelace to the clipboard. *Don't go there again.*

Even though I, a young woman, stood before her, aware I was a criminal culprit, I felt activated by her unapologetic feminism. It was inspiring, very much in the vein of what Maxine argued earlier that day at the workshop, that men were proponents of female hysteria.

Daniel, in contrast, wasn't a mark of that phenomenon at all.

Seeing how earnestly he wanted to be by her side broke my heart. It didn't feel like a personal betrayal that he wanted to be with her over me.

Instead, my heartache toward him showed me I still

had empathy. I recognized how defeated he must have felt. As the chaos settled down, I saw the ingenuity of his woe. He embodied the opposite of the EMT's critique. A pinnacle of male tenderness. That day, his persona sloped from a strong, grown man to a tearful, worried child. He faced firsthand the peril of someone he loved.

Daniel adored Maxine. Over the weeks, I'd observed his genuine admiration of her. The extent to which his work, just like mine, had been influenced, shaped, and inspired by her at her height.

One of my favorite qualities about him was his disregard for optics. He felt for others deeply, both in their excitements and their ailments. His emotions were clear. Unadulterated woe. Nothing to perform, nothing to disguise as strength.

Two policemen at the scene offered to drive us home and blasted the heat while we sat silently in the back, plagued by dark daydreams. I squeezed Daniel's hand in the middle seat throughout the ride, glancing his way occasionally, but he was off in a dark daydream. I wanted to hold him, kiss him, and tell him he had nothing to hide in my presence.

The squad car's heater hummed against the rain drumming on the roof. Each streetlight we passed cast Daniel's face in momentary amber before plunging it back into shadow. His hand felt cold in mine, still trembling slightly. Water soaked from his hair into his collar. The wet denim of his jeans left dark patches on the vinyl seat.

Clouds continued drizzling.

Images of the city flashed past us like a film reel. We found ourselves in some depressing, avant-garde stop motion picture. One of the cops had a Thermos filled with coffee, still steaming from the early morning. He flipped the lid and poured it into a cup. We passed it back and forth between us, watching as the windows condensed with steam in the rapid pacing of our breath.

Daniel's teeth had stopped chattering, but his shoulders occasionally shook with leftover adrenaline. His knuckles were white where they gripped the Thermos. I noticed a scratch on his palm from where he'd grabbed something—a rock, a branch, anything—trying to reach Maxine.

My socks were full of sand. I removed them in the back seat and watched as the specks scattered across the floor mat. I apologized through the partition, and he assured me it was the least of his worries. He was just glad everyone was okay.

He said when he arrived and saw how far she was in the water, he felt sure she'd met her fate. He'd seen a lot of death in the lake, and it kept him up at night. Daniel listened with empathetic sadness, grateful to commiserate.

I held my head down and felt regret starting to fill me. I asked myself why I couldn't just let it happen, why I became susceptible to fight-or-flight. My supernormal vigor, it turned out, wasn't enough to face human instinct. My critique of the curse was that, in crisis, my unconscious actions were to stay alive and protect.

I kicked myself. A shift in the curse's mechanics I didn't expect. It never occurred to me that I'd be at the behest of survival skills. I thought I'd packed up my need for survival and put it into storage. They should have been in the same vacuum-sealed plastic bin as my sympathy. Shut airtight with my baby blankets.

There's no reason this stuff should have been able to escape and find me. I didn't want it here. I didn't want Maxine to survive or, worse, make me feel sorry for her. It could rot in storage and get donated once I died for all I cared. I'd have to adjust as necessary.

ACT II: SCENE IX

Daniel and I stood in the doorway, kicking off our cold, wet sneakers. The dampness made his feet numb, and mine were also chilled. I clutched both pairs of socks in my hand. He apologized as he started removing his clothes.

He left his boxers on but was naked otherwise. I picked the clothes up off the floor and turned on the kettle. I grabbed a soft, fresh blue blanket and wrapped it around him like he was a baby. He held it tight and collapsed into a fetal position on the couch, teeth chattering.

In the mudroom at the back, I shook out his soaked jeans and sweater and set aside laundry detergent. I told him to take a hot shower while I made lunch for us, then disappeared to the bathroom to turn on the water. Maxine all but disappeared from my mind. Then, I became focused on playing house with Daniel. I felt eager to rehabilitate and care for him. I wanted to make him feel comfortable in my home.

The ceiling groaned as brown line trains passed and passed with weekday commuters. The unsettling rattle never failed to comfort me, a reminder that our world was a harbor of the unpredictable.

In the bathroom, steam clouded the mirror. I laid a fresh towel across the sink and returned to his side, inching close to his face while I swung his arm around my shoulder and led him to the tub.

DANIEL

Can you sit here with me? I'll leave my boxers on like a swimsuit. I don't want to be alone.

COREY nods and helps him in.

COREY

Is the temperature okay?

DANIEL sits on the bathtub floor in a ball, his head on his knees. COREY pulls the curtain closed and shuts the toilet lid, sitting on it beside him.

They're in a cocoon of white noise, water on water.

DANIEL

She's right about one thing. The world is dark and strange. Maybe not to the extent that she thinks, but don't you agree there's some truth to it all?

COREY

Maybe she lost it, but in many ways, she hasn't. Maxine is

an intuitive person. I'm sure all those feelings reflect some
sort of truth.

DANIEL
What is she already taking?

COREY
Valium, for sleep.

DANIEL
Was it helping?

COREY
It seemed to be. Then again, maybe not.

DANIEL
What next? Does she go on antipsychotics? What if they
change her?

COREY
They very well could. But listen, it isn't forever. She
should take the side effects a hundred times over her
current state.

DANIEL
I don't want to lose her.

COREY
You won't.

DANIEL
But I don't want to lose her in a spiritual sense, either. I
want her to stay the same.

COREY

I know, Daniel, but she's sick. You haven't seen the big picture. I've had more time to process living with her and the pacing of it all. It wasn't as sudden as it must have felt from your perspective.

Silence.

DANIEL

Do you think I gaslit her?

COREY

I've blamed myself, too. This is in no way your fault, nor is it mine.

Beat.

Do you want noodles?

DANIEL

Are you going to have some?

COREY

Yes. I like mine with a fried egg.

DANIEL

I do, too. Corey, despite it all, I'm glad you're here. I'm so happy I met you.

COREY

You, too.

The irony wasn't lost on me. I felt sorry for him, torn by the relief from our mutual affection and the heartache of seeing him in such distress. Guilt that I was the cause of his sorrow plagued me. Still, I saw how it drew him to me more and wanted to stay present in our special bond.

I also pulled my knees to my chest, struck by the moment's intimacy. A man sat vulnerable on the other side of the curtain, entrusting me with his doubts. My skin tingled with the wonderful agony of our newfound bond, the evocative setting.

After he shut off the water, I wrapped the towel around him like a hug. In the drawers somewhere, I had gym shorts and a T-shirt big enough to fit him. An added benefit of our shared small height.

Our faces were so close that our noses nearly touched. An echo radiated through my entire body. Echoing and echoing. I almost felt woozy. I found a faded Modest Mouse concert souvenir shirt and a pair of basketball shorts in my room. I cleared my throat and told him to lie down if he needed to, so I placed fresh clothes and socks at the edge of the bed.

While he changed, I fried two eggs and filled two bowls with buttered linguine. I placed the egg on top of the American cheese. Maybe he would laugh at me for that, but that's how I've liked it since I was a little kid.

Returning to my room, I found him on his side under the blanket. I placed the bowls on the nightstand to cool. He lifted the blanket like a door for me to enter. He looked helpless and in need of affection.

I hesitated, not wanting to rush things, but slid right in. Our chests pulled together in a magnetic field. They rose and fell with our breathing, now touching one another's surface. Then, I felt my heart open like a doorway. It let in a part of his soul that entered and disappeared, traveling deep into my core.

My breathing stilled. His eyes stayed on mine as if we couldn't move. I closed mine and willed a piece of my soul to send back to him. I watched the muscles in his face relax as he received it. From the beginning, I felt the currency was set in stone. It was a fact. We moved closer in. Our noses, our bellies, our laps, even our knees. Wherever we could make contact, we did. We kissed and kissed.

ACT II: SCENE X

The parochial school.

I spent the few days leading up to our next meeting fantasizing about Daniel like a schoolgirl. I touched myself thinking about the thrill of our most PG moments.

Our bellies brushed, how cute he looked in my old Modest Mouse shirt, how we slurped up pasta and cackled while commiserating about the bizarre nature of the whole day. *How had we started at an owl hole and ended up in the back of a cop car?*

We cackled about the most absurd details. Latching onto anything. Why did that cop give us his Thermos? When did Max become an Olympic swimmer? By the time we hit the details about the angry feminist EMT, I was crying with laughter. It had all been so serious, yet so strange. You couldn't make this up.

He beat me to our scheduled workshop and waited in the room for me with his arms long, his mouth wide open.

He finally heard from the hospital about how Max was doing.

Bam! Popped me like a balloon. I resented her stupid survival. *Yay.*

Maxine didn't call Daniel directly, but the nurse passed along a message in which Max thanked him for saving her life. Secondly, she wanted to tell him she felt anxious about the circumstances and how they could affect the timeline and financing of her residency. Daniel said the nurse assured her a medical emergency wouldn't bar her from success and, as her friend, he was honored to save her life, and she shouldn't worry.

Maxine reached out to her parents to share what had happened. They offered to come, but she insisted that they didn't. Daniel wasn't surprised. From what he knew after many years of context, her parents were lifelong tyrants with unrealistically high expectations. There was no way she'd sign a Release of Information for them, but she assured them she was in good hands. Her broken relationship with her parents worked well in my favor. I snooped in her documents under the guise of the worried roommate, knowing her isolation from family meant more opportunities for me. Daniel was relieved by Maxine's decision to write him in instead. He admitted that for days, he'd been afraid he was a source for her spiral, scared she would never forgive him. He assumed that my inclusion in the ROI was implied. I doubted that was true. She'd probably grown suspicious of me by then. Either way, I hated how she signed a ROI for Daniel and not for me, her roommate, who had taken care of her up to this point.

Why! I needed to alienate Maxine and Daniel from one another, not allow the trauma to bond them closer.

What possessed Maxine to cut me out of the equation? Had a vision pointed toward me as the villain? It was a life-or-death matter that I never got revealed. I did not pity her. I hated her. All my empathy was reserved for Daniel, and she was a bugging wasp. He presented the report.

DANIEL

I imagine you're subtextually included in this. But just in case, maybe don't mention it? The last thing I need is to break her trust while things are so precarious. But it is in her best interest, right? That her roommate knows what's up? Whatever. Anyway.

Daniel's brash justifications for the full disclosure made me wonder. When we traded a piece of our soul, did he inherit some of my evil? What if I'd corrupted him? I curled my toes, delighting even in the possibility.

I swore. The record was as follows.

Patient Overview:
The patient, Maxine Due, is a forty-four-year-old college professor, as well as a professional playwright and theatre director.

Reason for Visit:
Emergency services were called by Daniel Cho (the patient's Emergency Contact) and Corey Cordele (the patient's Roommate) as Maxine experienced a public episode at the lakeside and swam into dangerous water.

Affect at Arrival:
Upon admittance, the patient exhibits hyperactive, inappropriate, and aggressive behavior. Due to the severity of the agitation, medical staff administered a Geodon

(Ziprasidone) injection. Once aware, Maxine agreed to voluntary admittance for further observation.

Neurological Diagnosis:

None. Patient's CT scan was clear.

Psychiatric Diagnosis:

Unspecified psychotic disorder Maxine doesn't exhibit evidence to diagnose bipolar disorder or schizophrenia, as listed by the symptoms in the DSM-5. Maxine shared an off-and-on history of depression. She may exhibit Major depressive disorder with psychotic features.

Psychotic Symptoms:

Hallucinations and delusions: The patient's description indicates spiritual psychosis. Emphasis on interference from malicious entities, as well as a string theory of two timelines. The first, the world as we know it and the second, a nautical planet. She expresses psychic intuition, which enables her to visit both timelines. The patient describes messages from the nautical planet that tell a story about a curse instigated by a liaison of the devil.

Progress in Care:

The patient is eating at appropriate times, sleeping through the night, and participating in music, art, and therapy activities. She is friendly and appears to be creative, intelligent, and motivated. The patient seems to respond well to the prescribed medications.

Rx Prescriptions:

Ambien (Zolpidem: Sedative hypnotic)

Abilify (Aripiprazole: Atypical antipsychotic)

Seeing her progress, I wanted to barf. I could picture it so clearly: Professor Due, against all odds, continued to be everyone's favorite. She didn't even have to woo others with her charisma, but she tried, anyway. I hated how she insisted on being the varsity team captain of likeability. It was triggering me. The details too closely resembled what had led me to place the curse in the first place. Screw her.

DANIEL

Mostly good news. I'm thankful. This is the first sign that everything will be alright, and I can start normalizing what happened. Poor Maxine. She's experiencing a stigmatized health crisis, and it's no different from experiencing a freak accident. Plus, she'll get a ton of support from us here. We did the right thing.

COREY

I'm eager to see how it goes.

Beat.

DANIEL

Beyond this, I confess. I can't think straight. Not because of Maxine, but because of me and you.

The change of subject was thrilling. Like I said, when we joined souls in my bed, I hoped to awaken something dormant in him. A beautiful darkness he kept in a cage like a caught, wild animal, a thing he took no responsibility over. Now, hopefully, his animal recognized its mate in me, and he could be set loose.

He didn't have to pretend with me. No need to be a cautious mentor or a responsible artistic director. His hunger was so obvious because it mirrored mine.

DANIEL

Corey, I really can't stop thinking about you.

COREY

You, either.

COREY bites her lip.

DANIEL

I'm such a cliché. Is it wrong? Not because I don't want to be around you. God, I want it. I'm supposed to oversee your work here. We haven't even touched our work today. There's the crisis of Maxine, sure, but. . . the other stuff, too? I feel guilty, but I like it.

COREY

What do I care about ethics? We share the same opposition to the performative.

DANIEL

I know you do. But what about your age, too?

COREY

Don't baby me. I'm a grownup. You didn't say I was young, remember? I did.

DANIEL

Well, you are, but it's not what draws me in.

COREY

This has been inevitable from our very first emails. Couldn't you feel it then?

DANIEL

I did. Right away. You've shown me parts of myself I
didn't even know were there. You're not a tool for self-
recognition—but you are that, among many other
crazy, synchronistic, kaleidoscopic wonders. You're
truly. . . just awesome. I can't even believe you
like me.

COREY

Why wouldn't I like you? Look at you. Look at me

*COREY gestures between them, sitting in jeans, gray
jackets, and baseball caps.*

We're cut from the same cloth. It was only a matter of
time before we found one another.

DANIEL

I never, *never ever*, dove headfirst into something like this.
I don't know what to make of you.

*DANIEL takes off his ball cap, then, trying to secretly
smile at it, fidgets with it in his hands nervously.*

Plus, we kissed! What's up with that?

COREY

That was cool. That was nice.

DANIEL

You've shown me a sense of play I didn't know I was
missing. Over time, I'd gotten so serious. I'd lost the plot. I

forgot the clown in here even existed. I met you and knew I needed to brush up on my magic tricks.

The crucifix loomed over us, but it didn't bother me. I realized then that I'd integrated evil into myself. I viewed it without judgment as a special trait or skill. As Daniel put it, in the dark side, I found a sense of play I'd been too scared to explore before. I wanted to push it further and deeper. I wanted—

> DANIEL
> I want you.

DANIEL inches closer to COREY. She pushes a stack of pages out of the way.

> COREY
> What even is that?

> DANIEL
> It's your homework.

COREY smiles.

> COREY
> Yeah? And what is this?

COREY sits on DANIEL's lap, facing him.

> DANIEL
> Oh my god.

COREY kisses him.

COREY
What is it?

DANIEL
Recognition.

He grabbed a fistful of my brassy hair. Up close in the light, I noticed his freckles. His shiny, pitch-black hair, his pretty eyes. Daniel looked up at me then, really looked, and I saw the last threads of his resistance unravel. I'd be whatever he wanted me to be as long as I could be with him.

DANIEL
I see you. But Maxine will lose her mind.

COREY kisses him again.

COREY
I think she already has.

DANIEL
Maybe she has enough demons to battle. And with that—

DANIEL walks to the basement door and locks it. He turns off the work lights. Only the broken strand of Christmas lights remains.

I want to do something bad to you.

He took off his sweater and spread it on the floor, then wrapped his arms around my waist and pulled me in. The security of his strength was unexpected. My insides tingled. I released, entrusting him to take control.

His hands were rough against my skin, calloused from years of acrobatics and rigging. Each touch felt deliberate and practiced—the careful precision of someone who understood the mechanics of bodies in motion. The room's darkness made everything feel heightened and dangerous. The Christmas lights threw strange shadows across his face, making him look otherworldly.

I wondered how different this felt from our careful email exchanges and measured text messages. Here was the real Daniel. A human being. The basement's dank air pressed around us like a cocoon. Even Jesus averted his eyes, fed up with me, abandoning his vigilance.

The cold floor beneath his sweater grounded me while everything else felt surreal. His breath was warm against my neck. I could smell chalk dust in his hair and theatre wood in his clothes—the earthiness of someone who lived in these sacred spaces. The basement's usual creepiness transformed into something electrically arcane. He lowered me onto the sweater.

DANIEL

Do you remember that batshit thing Maxine said about time?

COREY wrinkles her nose and laughs.

COREY

How could I forget? *Time tries to terminate history.*

DANIEL

Yeah. Pretend it's true now. Not before this or after this.
Just this. This horrible, good thing.

He grabbed my face, and I closed my eyes. His aggression stopped my heart. Who needed a mask of normalcy when I belonged with Daniel, savoring these new feelings of shared, sacred sickness?

Our bodies met, and the universe contracted. We plummeted through an unreachable black hole beyond responsibility, consequence, and morality. We were only bodies, yet we were simultaneously bodiless, two twin creatures dissolved in the acid of this insatiable need, emerging on the other side as a single shadow.

ACT II: SCENE XI

By mid-November, Maxine looked fresh from the hospital's rest and self-care. Her bare, unblemished face had settled into an expression of intense wisdom, the new stress wrinkles giving her face the perfect added touch. She looked more grounded than I'd ever seen her, maybe even more real than before.

The hospital where she stayed was steps away from a train station, smack in the middle of a nice, bustling area with boutiques, ice cream parlors, and salons. She told me she'd been in the area a thousand and one times and couldn't believe, after discharge, that the psychiatric ward and the charming, busy, upscale block lived right down below. She described exiting the automatic sliding doors and entering the same city with a refreshed perspective.

At sign-out, the office manager on the floor encouraged her to find pleasure and confidence wherever she could. She took the advice seriously and stepped into a salon near the hospital. She said a brisk walk around the block did her good, too. Her main critique of the ward was that they weren't allowed outside.

Her stop included a clean-up cut, a wash and blow dry, and freshly filed nails. Nothing looked over the top. If anything, she looked understated, which made a world of difference to what had been broken.

She smelled like Dove soap and clean laundry detergent. She looked comfortable in a new set of fall clothes. Hydrated, moist, and fresh. She hadn't looked this good since the previous spring—and today, she even looked better than that.

MAXINE

Psychiatric care gets pigeonholed as if it's some flatly bleak, corrupt place. I'm certain it is that, but it can be other things, too. My experience as a recovering patient and an artist was enlightening. Meeting the other patients deepened my empathy. Now that I've seen into another universe, I'm optimistic I'll get well, but I also want to learn how to integrate these new spiritual takeaways into my work.

Her narrative of the experience hypnotized me. An outpouring of lovable, interesting characters. People who were manic, schizophrenic, the rich and the poor. Patients who admitted themselves and patients whose families admitted them. Some were angry, some frustrated, and some just felt lucky to be alive. Rich, homeless, it didn't matter. Society converged in the psych ward, she explained, one of the only places for people of real diversity to break bread together. Wearing the same uniform, sharing the same meals, and participating in the same activities.

She described the psych ward with cinematic detail—an elderly woman taking over the communal television with *Dance Moms*, a row of three curly-corded telephones in the middle of all the action—their only connection to the outside world. A man who tucked in the shirt of his hospital uniform formally. How he sat on the phone and shared whole, philosophical conversations with his wife who, Maxine heard at the community dining table, was long dead.

MAXINE

Corey, you wouldn't believe what people made in that place, not even if you saw it with your own eyes. I witnessed it firsthand, and I'm still grappling with it. Isn't it amazing how the people who have never been taught to paint or write are the ones who make the most amazing things? We really should look to them as a reference point.

Her favorite part was the library, which was only open for three hours daily. Rejuvenated by long, dreamless nights of sleep and the warm shell away from distraction, Maxine found a way to revive her research and writing.

MAXINE

The library had a few round tables and six rows of disorganized paperbacks. You wouldn't believe it. One of the books was about French folktales—a real coincidence —but a true one, not the psychotic sort.

COREY

Max, you were meant to be relaxing, not mastering my
research over me.

MAXINE

I relaxed. I swear! But you know me. I couldn't render
myself completely useless.

COREY shakes her head and rolls her eyes.

COREY

I can only imagine.

MAXINE

Want to know my biggest takeaway? Now, I'm wrestling
with different interpretations of psychosis. Many people
around the globe would *revere* it, and they are curious to
know more about the meaning behind the visions.
Many people don't view it as a sickness but an awakening
to admire.

Beat.

I don't want to be arrogant, though, and certainly do not
idealize my experience.
The levels of frightening shook me, and you know I have a
high tolerance.

Beat.

Anyway, food for thought. A compelling subject for
discourse. I know all the symptoms won't disappear for a
while, but I feel motivated to continue immersing myself

in these ideas. One day, I trust, they'll reemerge healthily in how I create and live my life.

I balked at it all. Seething. I couldn't compete with this crap. I couldn't tell if she competed with me or believed things would improve. Things would not improve. I wouldn't allow it. Yet doubt crept in. What if her story went even better than before this all started? I wanted to strangle her. I proposed my final resort for a win in that conversation.

COREY

Something enlightening happened to me, too.

MAXINE

Please. I'm very open to a change of subject.

COREY

Are you sure? I don't want to detract. Please don't judge me.

MAXINE

What is it?

COREY

I'm coming to you for advice and maybe validation. Since I met Daniel, he has been special to me. He seemed to be apart from everyone else.

MAXINE groans.

See? I knew how you would react. I know it's wrong, but I followed my heart. After you left for the hospital, we spent a few hours together. To my surprise, he felt the same, and we took. . . the plunge.

MAXINE
Are you kidding?

COREY
I was scared to tell you, but I can't change it now. We're too deep in it. It is what it is.

MAXINE pushes her thumb into the center of her brows, collecting herself.

Hello? Did I do something wrong? Do you have feelings for Daniel?

MAXINE laughs and sighs.

MAXINE
God, no. Are you kidding? For one, the circumstances are ludicrous. Who knows what could've happened to me? To think, I could still be there! Some people get trapped there for months, sick as dogs, with no solution in sight. What if I'd gone there and gotten worse? All while you two were, what, honeymooning? It's tone-deaf. To say the least. I'm certainly surprised.

COREY
It sounds to me like you're jealous.

MAXINE
That's fair. I'm jealous. But do you want to know what I'm jealous of? I'm jealous that you two didn't have to go

through what I did. I forbid myself to engage with those I'm supposed to protect. I'd never even allow myself to see Daniel like that, let alone act on it.

Beat.

As for your situation, it's a watering hole drama. It's no deterrent to me continuing to show up, give my all, and enjoy myself. I owe myself that. You won't win this one if you want me to be jealous. It'll run its course, anyway, and you'll see what a cliché you were.

COREY
How am I a cliché?

MAXINE
It cements what I tried to tell you in the first place: You're not ready for this. Now that you're here, realize that. You're engaging with social politics like a kid. You could easily set boundaries, yet you wasted perfectly good energy meant to be spent on your talent. Also, come on! Do you think he's unaware that you're young and probably more available than the women his age? As much as I love you as individuals, I don't know why you'd expect that to be lost on him.

COREY
Don't be mean. I can't blame you for your agitation and exhaustion, but you can't pretend to understand what you're not part of. You're still processing, learning to make sense of everything that happened.

MAXINE

It's the opposite. If anything, I'm feeling clearer than ever.

Daniel's fears of Maxine's side effects—apathy, slow bounce back, and the shakes—reflected her first day home as the opposite. Why was the opposite of his fear worse than the fear itself? I thought about attacking her. Gripping my hand around her neck while she faded, screaming in her face that I was the caster of the curse. I was the liaison of the devil.

It was explicitly clear the curse had broken. That, or it had turned on me. I had to go after Max as a human to execute all my plans. As mad as I was, I didn't want the supernatural to get to witness her suffering, anyway. I wanted pleasure. I wanted to write it from the first row with my hand. I deserved that. I wouldn't let her live forever like a vampire or let her die a martyr.

ACT II: SCENE XII

Over the next week, Maxine settled back into work with determination. The medications seemed to work, but something in her eyes had changed. The old Maxine performed in strength, but this Maxine inhabited it with an unsettling serenity.

I decided not to tell Daniel that I admitted his and my budding relationship to Maxine. I knew he'd blow it out of proportion with his concerns. His feelings were justified, given it was his duty to balance an already tender and precarious room, what with Maxine's leaving.

For her return, Daniel suggested we make it a special occasion and use the theatre's main stage instead of our usual basement room at the school. To him, it was important to reignite ours as a group with the proper gravitas.

I followed the idea and feigned enthusiasm the best I could. Truthfully, however, I hated being in the main theatre. I felt out of place there, taunted by the insecurities of pre-curse Corey, the version of myself who was young, stupid, and naive. The insecurities Maxine decided to willfully exacerbate in my own home upon her return from the psychiatric ward. She reawakened a former Corey, who I thought had died.

These insecurities set a new flame to my resolve to end her, however, whatever means it may take. As we entered the modern, feelingless cavern of the thrust stage, tiered with nearly nine hundred seats, nausea overcame me. Big, empty theatres set the stage for my nightmares. The enormous room was so sparse every word and movement echoed coldly. We'd been transported to the darkness of Antarctica during its season away from the sun.

Maxine sat down before me, still looking refreshed and composed under the influence of her new medication. For a moment, Maxine and I lived there as Daniel had disappeared into the light booth to turn on the circumstances for the horrific exercise to come. I carefully sat a few seats away from her to limit direct contact before the exercise started. While we waited for Daniel, I forced myself to focus on anything that could undercut the hurt and discomfort that stung inside me.

Moving inward, however, only exacerbated my spiral. I fell into deeper confusion, deeper anger. Encounters flashed within me, the lessons of each contorting. I felt removed from my grip on reality, subjugated by everything I had before interpreted as power. I felt dictated and suppressed by my own choices. Not only had Maxine scorned me, but she felt inspired to rise into an ethereal force of her own. Her visions gave her a momentary setback but resulted in more clarity. I wanted to kill her, but, freshly, I wanted to kill myself.

When I told her the news about Daniel and me, she delivered the worst punishment. Pity. There was no fight, no indication that her knowledge would change the dynamic of our trio, only my own pathetic, silent consequence of her disapproval.

When Daniel saw her, my insecurity was doubled down by how she greeted him happily, with no indication of something amiss. He remarked on how well she looked and clarified he didn't mean it to be patronizing and how seeing her restored to her former self made him radiate with even more possibilities of the directions the group would take. He said she should continue to take as much rest as she needed, to take space as often as she needed, and that he would support her success moving forward however best he could.

Maxine insisted upon being motivated and present, at least for the time being, because not only did she reground in her former self, but she'd evolved into something more. As tempting as it was for her to resent her experience, she told him she had to honor it and allow it to deepen who she was. Daniel nodded while listening to her tale, moved by how it all took shape.

I shook out the thought, centering back into the room. The architecture was crystal clean, grossly over-contemporary, and incapable of timelessness. It was built in a geometric balance that was too precise to withstand history. It was a caricature of itself, designed for the upper brow who funded it in the interest of glamor. The fancy executive board people would opt to donate to the cause of a fancy-lit sign or a coffee shop in the lobby rather than improving the nature of the art.

I just couldn't stand Maxine being back.

The sound of her fidgeting near me, organizing her

notes, and writing her stupid thoughts in her green pen infected me. Then, I was startled.

Daniel's voice boomed from the light booth through the main speaker from the stage manager's mic. He asked how it looked. My eyes went to the stage. A single, garish spotlight made a chillingly defined circle around two metal folding chairs that sat face to face.

Behind the chairs, a scrim extended across the stage, hung by a forty-foot baton. Projected onto the screen was the title of the exercise.

HOT SEAT.

The setup was meant to be an upgraded version of the GET THE SCARY OUT prompt. I missed the aging chalkboard. The perfectly spaced Serif font gave me goosebumps. I missed Daniel's handwriting. I missed the squeak of the chalkboard wheels, the remaining finger-prints of school children long past.

HOT SEAT was an exercise to help us better position ourselves in the theatre world. We were to answer a series of disciplined questions that moved through a pitch sheet. The questions covered our play concept, our dramaturgical source material, our vision, our budget plans, and our play title.

Daniel offered me the opportunity to go first since Maxine had just arrived again, and he wanted her to take her time and take it slow. In the HOT SEAT exercise, the artistic director was meant to sit further back in the theatre and was not allowed to comment on the interview live. He would be silently jotting feedback notes to give to the writer later.

That day, I'd sit in the writer's seat, and Maxine would sit in the interviewer's seat. Just what I needed— another opportunity for her to remind me of her expertise and teach me some degrading lessons. That was all she did, even when her operating system crashed. She was such a hypocrite. But she appeared to be at the height of her powers, and the pressure was nearly too much for me to endure.

Daniel exited the light booth and walked to the tenth or so row of the audience.

I searched for his smile, but he was lost in darkness. I wanted to feel his compassionate energy and receive a private nod, but all I could make out was his blank silhouette—a baseball cap and an oversized jean jacket. He asked us to go ahead onto the stage. As I arrived in the light, even his silhouette disappeared. My only proof he existed was a light flutter of notebook paper capped by the click of a pen. He was ready.

I shook as I sat.

Max's new authority radiated off her like heat. She glowed as she steadily walked from the front row onto the stage and sat in the interviewer's chair. Her black hair was a blast from the past, twisted up in a clip. Her tan linen jacket and pants looked pressed again, and her signature masculine oxfords clicked as she walked along. Her glasses hung on a chain around her neck.

She'd clipped the interview questions to a clipboard with some of her details written in the margins. She had over-prepared for her arrival back to the workshop. I had been underprepared for my interview. My heartbeat clashed and clamored. My bones chattered. I had no hope of restoring my confidence and focused solely on getting through it. The oncoming catastrophe was inevitable. Prodromal humiliation. There was no use crying out to the powers that be. They had forsaken me.

I crossed my legs back and forth, worried about

optics, the thing I hated the most. My skirt looked amateur. I worried my lipstick was crooked. I couldn't get comfortable. The chair leg felt cold on my calf. I couldn't release my trap. I pleaded for Daniel's help with my eyes, but there was only blackness. My only set pieces were two hostile chairs. Maxine cleared her throat.

MAXINE

Are we ready to get started?

DANIEL

Whenever you're ready, Max. Go ahead and start the time.

MAXINE picks up DANIEL's red egg timer, sitting at her feet, and sets it. COREY inhales once sharply through her nose, then leans forward.

MAXINE

State your name.

COREY

Corey Cordele.

MAXINE

So that we're clear on the structure, I will ask you a series of questions. You must answer each with secure confidence. Your role as a playwright is not to merely write. You must also pitch and defend your work. Answer the questions clearly without hesitation. You may not use filler words such as *like* or *um*. You are not here to finesse your play concept. You are here to prove you can conduct

yourself for an audience and potential producers. Are we
clear?

COREY *sighs.*

COREY
Yes.

MAXINE
What is the play about?

COREY
A medieval peasant, who, rather, goes to, um.

MAXINE
What is the play about?

COREY
A desperate peasant makes a deal with the devil. Then
she. She. I'm sorry. I'm trying not to say um.

MAXINE
Again.

COREY
An unsuspecting woman enters a rigged deal with the
devil. She's forced to live as a Siren for the rest of her life.

MAXINE
A Siren?

COREY
Sorry. A Mélusine.

MAXINE
What is the difference between a Siren and a Mélusine?

COREY
The latter has two tails.

MAXINE
Say more.

COREY
The Mélusine is usually depicted in freshwater.

MAXINE
Say more.

COREY
In several stories, for some reason, they're only a Mélusine
on Saturdays.

MAXINE
Why?

COREY
I'm sure it isn't arbitrary.

MAXINE
Are you sure? I don't understand. The difference between
a Siren and a Mélusine.

COREY
Mélusines are shapeshifters.

MAXINE
Sirens can be shapeshifters, too.

COREY
A Mélusine is on the Starbucks cup. Why are you taking
notes?

MAXINE
You aren't allowed to ask the interviewer questions.

COREY
It isn't your job.

MAXINE
These are for my reference. What is your research or
reference material?

COREY
Related mythology in Annecy, France.

MAXINE
What is the play trying to explore?

COREY
Subversion of myth. A concept artist designed a complex
multimedia installation—

MAXINE
No one cares.

COREY
I thought it was interesting.

MAXINE
That's very clear. What is your unique interpretation of your source material?

COREY
Fascination.

MAXINE
There's a glaring oversight in your research analysis.

COREY
What is the oversight?

MAXINE
You may not ask the interviewer questions. What is your unique interpretation of your source material?

COREY
It fascinates me. It. Um.

MAXINE
Again.

COREY
Can't you give me a break? I'm new to this. Daniel, can you help me understand what I'm missing?

MAXINE
He won't talk. That's the rule.

COREY
You tell me what, then.

MAXINE

Why refer to source material you don't understand?

COREY

Tell me what I don't understand.

MAXINE

No. You tell me.

COREY

I can't right now. I will have to revisit it.

MAXINE

Do you at least have a name for your play?

COREY

It's, um. It's. It's still a working title. *A Play About A Curse.*

MAXINE

A working title. A file name for a sixty-thousand-dollar grant. You are not ready for this.

The timer goes off.

The tears came flowing. I sniffled and rubbed my nose with my sweater. I looked at Maxine and bit my lip, crying harder. I shielded my eyes from the light, gasping, struggling to walk down the steps and through the aisle toward the back exit.

I could only see Daniel's eyes in the darkness as I passed him. He was busy writing furious notes but paused to look at me with pity. I refused to accept sympathy, not from him and not from anyone.

I pushed through the exit doors and beelined through the lobby, past a group of people getting a tour of the hideous theatre building, moving faster, shoving the glass entryway open, and hitting the sidewalk. I didn't stop moving, not for anything. I tightened the straps of my backpack while I went, picking up faster and faster, momentum only increasing as I zig-zagged through packs of slow walkers, faster than ever, even quicker than when I fled Maxine's wrath back in Dallas, when I arrived at the clairvoyant's den and placed the curse. That day, I fled with nothing. I ran toward something, hellbent on taking the opportunity into my own hands.

I arrived at Maxine's and my building, stormed through the entry, and ran up the flights.

ACT II: SCENE XIII

I dug my key into the lock and kicked the door open.

I didn't even bother kicking off my shoes or fiddling to get the keys out of the lock. I threw my backpack onto the floor and plowed forward, unstoppable. To the bathroom. To the control center of Maxine's newest success, the medicine cabinet.

The shower curtain moved slightly, either from the heater or in the angry rattle of my perception. The cabinet door hung crookedly. Its hinges creaked like the rigging of a noose.

I paused and stared in the mirror, seeing my whole self for the first time. I couldn't allow anything, not even the world's most sinister forces, to take credit for what I'd become. I was a thing to be feared. Ruthless on my own accord. Bad because I wanted to be bad. No one would dictate to me any longer. I didn't care how badly I hurt anyone.

There I was—humiliated, beautiful, hurt, betrayed—a work of art to be admired. The wet, red eyes added character. The nest of tangled, windblown hair added sex appeal. The flush of embarrassed cheeks decorated me with unabashed colors.

I shed the shame, leaning in as close as possible to my eyes. My touch, my electricity. It filled me with pleasure that was missing from encounters with other people. I wanted to grab my hair, kiss myself, and throw myself onto the floor helplessly. Submissive and dominant at the same time. Intermixing pleasure and plain. Touching myself with blood on my hands. Banishing myself to a void of isolation where I relished in everyone else's fear. I didn't want to be seen by anyone but me.

The fluorescent bulb above the mirror buzzed and flickered, casting a sickly green tint across my skin. Water dripped in tortuous, indiscernible rhythms. *Drop. . . drop drop drop. . . drop drop drop.* Erratic like my pulse. The air smelled of plastic-laden drugstore shampoo, immersing me through scent into the dynamic setting of a scary daydream.

The scene marked the end of my human relationships. I'd no longer bear responsibility for others' limitations and suffering. Everyone's pain was their fault. No one deserved anything. Everyone had missed out on the fun, the freedom of putting themselves first. But I discovered it.

I admired the fearlessness of my subversion. The cruelty in my eyes. The pursuance of the true avantgarde. The yearning so strong it could crack a rib. I swore never again to limit myself to the confines of the rehearsal room. The demands of artists to consent to the very systems they claimed to go against. The very idea of elevator pitches implied subjugation.

How dare the world boss us around to become products of perfection. Fuck the idea of alienation. Fuck the idea of discomfort. Fuck the whole phony grand scheme of all of it. The core of the theatre was all a ruse. I wouldn't subject myself to it anymore.

The hideous, scaled tiles pulsed with my rage. Everything was hyper-real—the slippery, puddled texture of the counter, the way my fingernails dug half-moons into my palms, the way I could taste crusted toothpaste just by seeing how it spilled out of the bottle in a spearmint blob.

When I leaned in close, the mirror's surface felt cool against my forehead. My breath left little clouds that disappeared and reformed. I slammed my fist on the sink and cried out to my reflection, *Have you been here this whole time?*

I dried off the counter to protect my medium of choice—pills. I twisted the lids, and pills tumbled out, clinking as they hit the counter. Each one identical, perfect, deadly in its sameness. The antipsychotics were slightly larger, with a faint line scored across the middle. The sleep medication was only a hint smoother. Together, they formed a pile of seemingly carbon-copy pills. I arranged them carefully, precisely, like I was setting up cards for a trick.

After I switched the medication, she would deteriorate throughout the ninety-day supply of the prescriptions. Side effects: flop-flipping. She'd go incoherent—a sedated subject of hypnosis by day and an elevated antipsychotic at night. My vision of her descent was fantastic. Her hallucinations and delusions would be exacerbated. Night terrors transposed into daydreams.

Her executive function would deteriorate. She'd move through the world in a state of disorganized hypnosis. The strengths of her medication and how well they sat with her would backfire spectacularly, splashing her with all the pain she put me through. But my pain was gone. I'd be gone, relishing in the horror that all these pretenders tried to convey.

I performed my final magic trick:

One hand over each of the piles of pills, rotating them. It's one of those tricks where you follow a coin placed under a cup, inevitably losing it. The audience of these magic shows can't see how the magician slips in and pulls the coin. Beneath the cups, there is no coin at all.

In my version of the trick, there were two coins. Both of which led to ruin. I recited the grave lists of side effects like spells. *Incoherence. Clumsiness. Mania. Confusion. Inappropriate affect. Aggressive behavior.* Then, the big finale.

Self-harm. Suicide.

She would never die a martyr. She would believe her inner shadow people and convince herself it was her idea, her inevitable choice to end the suffering. But it was all me behind the scenes all along.

Two of me stood there—one in the world and one in the mirror. Four hands, four eyes, two heads, two noses, and two mouths. All mine. I could've even grown a tail if I wanted it bad enough. My heart was a gulf of desire, an abyss of yearning.

I circulated the pills once more, enjoying the feeling of it, allowing myself to surrender to whatever strange form of pleasure that felt good.

The bottles made hollow plastic sounds as I refilled them. *Fall, clink. Fall, clink.* My calculated rhythm defied natural sciences. Every surface I touched received my energy. My fingerprints remained invisible on the outdated granite. The proof of what I'd done—camouflaged by a heinous speckled finish, written into history through a cipher only I could crack. I only had the landlord to thank for his penny-pinching and his refusal to refinish the bathroom.

I wormed the orange bottles back into the cabinet, one by one, just as I had found them. The light gave a loud, sharp buzz as I flicked off the switch. My reflection hid in the black before my eyes adjusted. There was only one unseen detail, hidden from the naked eye—everything had changed. Time wouldn't dare to terminate history, so I did.

And then, it was finished.

Blackout.

The End of Act II.

INTERLUDE: MAXINE

INTERLUDE: MAXINE

MAXINE

Hello, my name is Professor Maxine Due. I'm honored to be considered for the visiting playwright position at the conservatory here in Dallas. I was asked to prepare a five-minute lesson on a chosen subject for this final round of interviews. Today, it's my pleasure to discuss with you all: *WHAT DEFINES A PLAY?*

MAXINE pulls out an old-school lighting projector and turns it on, illuminating the scrim. In green handwriting, WHAT DEFINES A PLAY?

The answer depends on who you ask. Today, we'll look at the question through the lens of the great practitioner

Bertolt Brecht. In doing so, I'll cue in my interpretation from a unique point of view.

Brecht defines epic theatre as a performance that distances itself from the audience rather than drawing them in. In today's climate, it's common for audience members to ask themselves whether or not they see themselves in the character.

Shadows appear of people taking notes. Pen clicks. Jotting. An anxious squall. The room temperature drops.

Brecht might argue that the sentiment of relating to the character is trite. Morality is en vogue, but I find it a limited, self-infantilizing way to view a story. Instead, the theatre should create a gap between the audience and the story told before them. In the gap, there lies intensity. Brecht's theatre isn't meant to deliver a lesson but to incite philosophical reckoning.

MAXINE switches slides: DO YOU TRUST THAT THIS INTERLUDE IS REAL? WHY OR WHY NOT?

It isn't the theatre's job to make you feel good. Ask yourself. Why are you so obsessed with feeling good? If you want neat and tidy, stay in your bedroom where there aren't any contradictions around every corner. But even there, ask. Do you even relate to the character that is yourself?

MAXINE places a new slide sheet onto the projector: I STABBED MYSELF TO DEATH ON CHRISTMAS

EVE. The words about her suicide loom over her head. An unrealized prophecy.

My next question lies in these contradictions. When does a play end? Does a play end at the blackout? Does a play end when the set gets struck and stored in a warehouse? How about when the theatre shuts its doors?

Or does it go on past all of that? Does a play end when the playwright dies? Does it end when the last person who remembers it forgets? Or does the play go on forever?

MAXINE places a new slide sheet onto the projector: I'M NOT COMMUNICATING FROM THE AFTERLIFE. The projector's fan stutters briefly. The light flickers but reorients.

I believe a play goes on forever. Artists continue to contribute to the theatre even after they have passed. I believe plays and stories are told in the present tense because they exist in a world that is simultaneous to our world.

MAXINE places a new slide: AFTER DEATH, THERE IS NOTHING.

I'll be humble. I don't have a clear definition, but I think Brecht was onto something.

MAXINE pulls the final slide from the projector. A blank light. Then, disgusting black water bubbles up from the projector hole, puddling in a reflection across the scrim. It carries the thick, organic smell of a toilet. Of a lake bottom.

Of things lost to decay. It spreads in patterns that almost form words, then foams onto the floor. A failing sewage system, darkening the projector's light, widening into a pond across the stage. A static pop and a spark. The projector shuts off. She bows.

Blackout.

The End of MAXINE's Interlude.

ACT III: ANNECY

ACT III: SCENE I

Through December, Maxine's stability had taken on an eerie quality. She stopped talking about her visions and ostracized herself, spending most of her free time with the door closed.

People who weren't as close to her thought she deserved a break and rest from the hustle and bustle. Everyone saw it as a recovery. Only I seemed to recognize it for what it was. Maxine showed the terrible clarity of someone who'd made a final decision.

The wrong medications had done their work slowly, invisibly. What looked like healing was surrendering. Each day, she grew more remote, more certain, until that final week when she stopped fighting altogether.

On Christmas Eve, when Maxine finally died, I didn't feel the need to celebrate. I nearly felt nostalgic when I found her body stabbed through the gut and twisted across the bed. Sentimental about our relationship, I reacted with admirable tranquility.

The knife lay beside her, its wooden handle worn smooth from years in her kitchen drawer, transforming the mundane into the extraordinary one final time. Her silk pajamas, wrinkled from sleep, were wet with the blackening magenta of her blood. The bedsheets told the story of her last movements—how she'd curled inward like a comma, almost onto the next thing, then curled into a period. There was nothing more to say.

Her desk calendar was marked through December 24th. Each day's box contained neat bullet points—tasks completed until the end. The last entry read simply: *Study. Write. Make.*

The room had no note of explanation, no final message. Just the careful organization of someone who'd planned everything meticulously.

In her bedroom, on a dedicated shelf, I admired her souvenirs from her time in Texas. There was a pair of cowboy boots from fellow faculty with a note to remember them all when she was back in the Windy City. Sitting just beside it were thank you letters and congratulatory cards from students. There was even a greeting card from me. Ironically, it was a Christmas wish from the year before, when I was a senior. I gave her a card and a planted poinsettia, which she sat on her desk in her office, well into the next year, once all its crimson petals turned to the color of dust.

Abstract art and photographs decorated the walls, swirling canvases of cool yellows and warm blues. Playbills had been stacked in the seat of a tan tweed chair, a comfortable place to sit in the morbid scene. Mountains of fuzzy linens and oversized pillows surrounded her body.

A cedar candle crackled on the night table, its strong woody scent destined for a transition into the new year. In other circumstances, her settled-in den placidly separated from outside disturbance.

I absorbed that tranquility she left behind. Her death didn't give me any fresh excitement. Only a quiet, reflective feeling of relief. I calmly called the emergency services. The policeman looked at me sadly and affirmed to me the grief of my loss. He said he'd seen more suicides around the holidays than at other times of the year. To him, it was evidence of the grave loneliness that prevailed through mankind.

Cleaning up the scene, I used a medicine dropper to extract a trace of Maxine's blood to carry in a vial to feed the monster at Lake Annecy. Although I felt forsaken by the forces behind the curse, I promised to uphold my end of the bargain. More than that, I needed to find answers at the source.

In the death scene, Maxine's face stays blank and vacant. I left her eyes open, red and swollen, and almost expected them to blink. I pulled fresh, folded, heirloom washcloths from a stack on the nightstand and used them to absorb the blood. I thought of all her family members using them to wipe their mouths during dinner, clean the kitchen countertops with baking soda and lemon juice, and press them to their foreheads during bubble baths.

If I were her family, I'd hate hearing it. I discarded the drenched, dripping rags and never told a soul. Her blood was the same quality as the stuff of the sewers. Glorified, ethereal trash.

I texted Daniel only once after her death. I asked if he remembered his question to me during late summer when he asked for my take on Modest Mouse touring after a core band member had died.

He responded, *Well? What do you make of it?*

I bought a one-way ticket.

In January, the air in Annecy stayed between thirty and forty degrees. Even though I was new, I could see how life in Annecy continued as it had without me, on and on, with mechanical precision. Shop owners shaped their displays long before dawn in the same manner their families had used for centuries.

Children walked to school through narrow passages, their backpacks bouncing against stone as they brushed it. The walls had been present through countless wars and triumphs. Rivers and lakes stayed in predictable rhythms. Tide at dawn, fishing boats at eight, tourist pedal boats out by noon.

These routines were an insult to Maxine's inevitable exit. While I tracked the hours through coffee cups and newspaper deliveries, my mind kept returning to that final scene. The careful way she'd folded her clothes on the chair showed me she'd found balance and clarity in her end. The disarray of the curse's early mania had become a resigned ritual. Her planner's last green check mark is as if it will continue no matter what.

Annecy lived forward, but I kept looking back, unable to make sense of her departure. After I switched her medications, I lost control of the plot.

The Alps stood stark white against the sky. I rode my rented bike past alternating patches of brown winter grass and white frost. The cold air stung my lungs as I pedaled uphill.

In the countryside's farms, blue shutters lined the windows, along with red geraniums that survived the winter. The cobblestones had been worn down over centuries, turning slick with ice where the sun couldn't reach.

In the cafés, espresso steam rose from tiny cups. The bakeries produced fresh baguettes every hour. I cracked finger-sized holes in the crust and wedged them in balls of fresh butter. At the outdoor markets, vendors arranged salamis and prosciuttos in neat rows. The sharp scents of cheese intermingled with sweet brioche.

I indulged in the grounded, sensory pleasures of the physical body. In Sanskrit, what yogis call the annamaya layer is known as the sheath of food. Muscles, connective tissues, and the most real human nervous-system-driven impressions of tickles, itches, and tastes. Annecy's fresh water tasted mineral-rich and was cold enough to hurt my teeth. Winter ducks left V-shaped ripples in the lake that pointed inward toward the shore.

In the evenings, cooking smells from restaurants and homes drifted down narrow streets. There was a lull after the workday, and then the streets bustled with people. Garlic-marinated steaks from French kitchens mixed with Aperol and elderflower liqueur. The medieval prison in the moat's center cast a shadow that reoriented around the room.

At the end of my chapter in Chicago, I felt the beginning of an ascension into something more. But for the time being, during my trip to France, I inhaled steam rising from my espresso. I tasted the subtle, creamy brie flavor as it melted into the crisp folds of a fresh baguette. I recalled my amateur associations with France without self-judgment. Running and biking through trails, the muted rainbow of winter in the Alps flashed around me between patches of frosted grass.

The yolky yellow centers of edelweiss, dark columbine's graying violet, and deep fuchsia pom-poms of vanilla orchids. I moved vigorously, embracing every bruise and spot of mud that appeared on my calves. My palms became as calloused as the circus performers' due to how firmly I gripped the handlebars. I rode and ran until I tired, collapsing into fields around rainbow rural farms. Parasailers soared above me one by one, other people who tested the boundaries of human nature through flight.

Mornings in Annecy were the best part.

But then, one morning, I fell privy to physical discomfort. I noticed myself perspiring more than ever, sweating through my winter clothes and digging through baskets of mixed fruits at the farmer's markets. My hair grew long during hyperfocus and neglect. A cardigan hung pointlessly around my waist, the veins in my torso spotty with chills. I was cold and hot at the same time.

Then, I recognized the limits of human nature not as forces to bore us to tears but to set challenges for us. Reading as I sat along the sides of medieval cobblestone surrounding bookshops and bakers, I felt like a wise, aging Princess Belle, her aching motivation to ascend from provincial life and indulge in the curiosities of an anthropomorphic castle where she became one with the Beast.

I printed Maxine's plays as reading material. I departed from her signature green ink and decided on magenta for myself. I saw magenta as nonconformity, transformation, and a wild sense of willpower. Rich and flexible between three shades. A force of a liaison between pink, red, and purple. A renegade.

I wrote in the margins just as she had done on my writing for years. I drew hearts around lines that made me laugh, question marks around ones I felt were unclear, and underlines beneath moments that weren't working. I scribbled my opinions of how she could have improved the work, but admittedly, her writing was nearly flawless. Even after her death, I felt desperate to prove her wrong about something, but even postmortem, she continued to hold some elusive knowledge over my head.

I obsessed about what Max meant in the HOT SEAT. What was the glaring oversight in my research? It haunted my every thought. While I pursued basking in my physical body, the psychological haunting of my *glaring oversight* bothered me more than any interference from the devil. It picked and picked at me. Maxine's callousness stood as the immortal, rooted in the French *immortalité*.

Despite my many transcendences, I feared Maxine was the immortal femme fatale while I was stuck playing the peasant. I felt glued to the ground, haunting the land like the dead characters of *Our Town*, wishing I could eliminate myself and become a spirit, satisfied even with a lack of an answer.

I walked along and ate pears, the smell of bitter Robusta beans and apricot poppies guiding me. Coolers crowded with fresh-laid eggs and gruyère, enticing loud groups of families and friends. Like me, a few loose chickens wandered down the path, going nowhere. I pushed lightly through the people—they were all untroubled, meandering on a sunny afternoon. I didn't understand their happiness—the darkness stayed in place at my strict instructions. Over the weeks, my withering desire to be one with the world cemented that I was separate, growing increasingly overstimulated. The world was a cave of unbearable noise. But I needed to ensure that my choice to go to Annecy couldn't be seen as fleeing from something.

Maxine's and my entanglement didn't go by the book. It was being rewritten at such a rate my hand couldn't keep up. I told myself a story that the curse wasn't failing. It was evolving.

I hoped soon it would open like a gate into paradise.

ACT III: SCENE II

I settled into an inn, the unassuming Hôtel du Château, just down a hill from Annecy's large center castle. Like the Chicago parochial school, a spinoff of the glamorous main theatre, the Hôtel du Château was a rickety mom-and-pop.

The small hotel was the most affordable in town. I was no longer working for pay. Our promised one-year residency was decapitated in just four months, from Maxine's psych ward stay through my leave to her final exit. None of it mattered now. I was done with Chicago, theatre, and everything but my promise to give back to the curse. The board decided to provide me with half of the grant. I knew the half-sum wouldn't get me through a year. I took it as a deadline, whittling away.

My most prized possession—a wad of blood money.

The hotel's floors creaked underfoot, scattered with a hodgepodge of rugs. Dust caught the weak winter light coming through the windows. The record player in the community room made a distinct mechanical sound before playing. The curtains smelled like stale potpourri. The bed and breakfast area seemed set up for a messy family reunion, with easily washable linens that doubled as dish rags.

The building was a mid-century contrast to the castle's austerity. A bienvenue sign greeted the front lobby, where I'd ding a little bell and wait patiently for the owners or attendants, who always seemed to be on break. The stereotype of the European mindset rang true—bask fully in life's pleasures during our limited time on Earth. They came and went as they pleased but left a pot of peppermint chocolates for guests to enjoy while we waited. I, an American, tried not to ask too many questions to not waste time.

Shelves of dusty books made a perimeter around the community room. The library reminded me of the one Maxine described in the psych ward. She'd said the limit there was three hours, so I followed the model and set timers for three hours with breaks for walks and deli visits in between. I took three hundred pages of notes in a month.

In the study spiral, I found a laser-sharp focus on my research about the history of Annecy. Across the Atlantic Ocean, far from America, stood the great castle—Le Château d'Annecy.

It loomed over the world in eerie glory. The timeless heaven of my wildest dreams. Built meticulously over an extended series of years between the twelfth and sixteenth centuries. But the project was never done, not really. Annecy's residents tinkered and fiddled with edits to it, no matter how much time had passed.

I read about how the castle preserved and reflected elements of medieval and Renaissance architecture. For a few hundred years, it housed Geneva dukes and duchesses, but as far as I knew, it was cursed. It burned down again and again, its resurrections moving in a wheel.

At some point, the builders threw their hands up in resignation. They gave up and left the castle vulnerable to Alpine overgrowth, prepared to burn as nature demanded. But it kept attracting people who had new visions, visitors from all over the world.

Those like me, who were interested in the castle's history, felt the structure had been misused and even mistreated. As time passed, locals insisted the abandoned barracks actively resisted the myths and fables surrounding Annecy's culture. Unlike the human wars the castle had come to represent, most Annecians were mystified instead by another world in Lake Annecy, the great turquoise body of water the castle overlooked.

I embodied their obsession, fixated on the dozens of gory allegories and fables from the canon of Haute-Savoie. Fantastic tales of mermaids and blood-curdling threats of Sirens prevailed in the region.

The culture evolved and imprinted the region, and future cultures would continue making their marks. Close by, in Switzerland, Le Château de Chillon inspired King Triton's castle in Disney's *The Little Mermaid*. The castles' very structures responded to elements of underwater mythology—their cores solid, unabashedly unwavering, resigned to existing in the imaginary waters above land so fires couldn't catch them.

At last, the books led me to modernity, when the Ministry of Culture purchased the castle of Annecy and made a museum. The museum was home to a remarkable collection of highly sought-after relics.

It held Medieval and Renaissance paintings, Catholic art, and eons of hand-carved wooden furniture. But even with the impressive permanent collection, my real interest was in the rotating exhibit—particularly Joan Fontcuberta's series, *Sirens*. His work was the impetus for my visit.

I was determined to visit once I felt spiritually ready. And until then, I worked myself to a decaying bone. My physical appearance deteriorated. Chapstick couldn't save my fraying lips. The stubborn, never-ending push of running and biking every spring took a toll on my body.

My hands cracked like the skin of a reptile's as I read and hand-wrote frantically. Soon, my vision blurred, so I went to the pharmacy to get a pair of reading glasses. I became disinterested in hygiene as I hyper-fixated on what I was *missing*. What was it? Was I stupid? I had no reason to fear physical ugliness or pain. It'd be an arrogant rant, lost in the grave swirl of sadness of human existence.

Pillow creases stayed imprinted on my cheek until noon. Indigo ditches sank deep beneath my eyes. My voice was hot and husky, and every inhale and exhale made a little click. My hair tangled into a ball and went brittle. When I ran my fingers through it, strands came loose. It hung in separate clumps instead of its usual waves. The color dulled from brass to dishwater. Bruises continued to appear without reason. My knuckles swelled until they became round.

Before I knew it, my posture curved inward like a question mark. Even shirts hurt my shoulders. My collarbones grew outward like a shelf on top of my torso. Every rib could be counted.

I became ancient, a configuration of skeleton and muscles at its very worst form. My joints snapped when I sat. Walking upstairs required rests between floors, my breath coming in short gasps. The hotel stairs that once took seconds started demanding minutes. My every step was halted by a brutal pause.

It was all Maxine's fault!

But I would take my physical descent a hundred times over not finding the answer, not being right. Fogs of headiness replaced my early human interest in Annecy. Over the weeks, my physical body all but disappeared. I stopped eating and watched bones emerge, replacing my muscles. I got the shakes. I survived on espresso and cocoa. Eventually, my hands became so frail I switched to a keyboard, but they failed me there, too. When I typed, my hands trembled along the keys, smashing too many at once or missing them entirely.

After a bit, my writing was reduced to turning on the same crooning French record, staring out the window down the hill, and treating the community center as a living room.

Hardly anyone spoke to me. I made little effort to practice French with the people and became an American loon. The stinkier my breath got, the more I smelled like mildew, and the more my hair rebelled, the more the owners began to question how long I would stay there. They were polite, insisting I was welcome for however long, but their judgment and disdain were obvious.

The library's reading lamp cast jaundiced, hollow shadows into my face. My unwashed hands left oil prints on the pages. The chair's cushion went flat from my hours of sitting. Wine glass rings stained the wooden table. My serrated fingernails caught on the paper as I flipped and flopped. Bits of my skin snagged on rough page edges. Paper cuts stung my dry rashes.

A homemade wooden bed was adorned with heart-shaped pillows in my sleeping quarters, underlining my loneliness. I caught myself missing Daniel, touching myself occasionally to the morning when he laid me on the parochial room floor. Flooded again with hatred and detestation, I adopted the sexuality of a rabid raccoon. Nothing was left to be desired.

My reading glasses pressed red marks into my nose. My room smelled mucky. I only had a sliver of soap and was out of fresh towels. I forbid the staff from entering my room for a refresh. I defended it like a hawk from intruders. I kept the room under my watchful eye but lost track of myself.

Sweater sleeves looked like hoop skirts around my narrow wrists. The waist of my jeans made ripples where I cinched the denim with safety pins and cut my hips. Stiff, unwashed piles surrounded me. The few belongings I had were treated like trash. They weren't my work, and they meant nothing.

At night, heart-shaped pillows from my bed were scattered on the floor. The wooden headboard creaked whenever I shifted position. Through the thin walls, I could hear other guests making love.

I kept the small perfume jar of Maxine's blood at my bedside with a tall, green candle I refused to light. In the Alps, I picked a fistful of yellow winter jasmine and scrunched it into a knotted bouquet. I didn't bother putting it in water and watched it die like a live production as I lay on my side with the cold window open, unable to sleep.

I saw my deterioration as a phase of transience. The

metamorphosis demanded physical sacrifice. The bodily atrophies were discouraging, but I trusted every putrefaction marked progress toward a higher state. Inside, my organs continued to shift and shuffle, rearranging themselves for some new form. My heart galumphed in strange rhythms. The transformation made my skin turn inward, preparing the shell for something else. My body could be as cruel to me as it wanted, and I wouldn't relent until I was done. The inner workings of fate had long been reconfigured, so I waited patiently.

When I knew I was closing in on the end of my capabilities, I clutched my back and limped up the hill to the Château d'Annecy, where the archaeological exhibit lived —the one that spiked my interest, but Maxine claimed wasn't hooky enough.

Inside, I traveled upward through winding staircases, every floor a planet, exhibitions of ancient and modern art, multimedia scenic displays of antique furniture, film, and collage. I strained my lungs, hobbling up the steps and stopping to sit on benches in dark corners.

Each floor had its own temperature and smell. The ancient artifacts smelled like wet pennies, while the modern art rooms smelled like vinegar and orange oil. The stained-glass windows cast colored shapes on the brick. My footsteps echoed differently everywhere I walked.

I gasped as I clutched my aching hip. Every muscle was tight and decrepit. I looked like and believed myself to be an old hag. I averted mirrors, not out of shame but out of determination. Against all odds, I would find the answer to what I was missing.

I'd nearly reached the top when I threw my hands in the air and groaned loudly to myself. People passing by looked at me with concern, asking if I was alright, but I shouted at them to piss off. Disgruntled, I had nearly fled the maze before I found myself in a cool, dark, modern room at the top of the castle.

Curators moved quietly between glass cases with their clipboards. Their shoes squeaked on the polished floor. The nautical displays cast blue-tinted reflections. Warm light flickered above the glass cases, sparkling through the dim air.

On the floor, there was a mix of art and administrative offices. Historians and curators mingled with clipboards, chattering about how to administer the preservation of the city, which they abided by like an art form of its own.

Nautical art surrounded me in every direction. Models of ships and diagrams of the moats and the great Lake of Annecy nestled into the mountains. I staggered to a large, archeological glass case where I saw it—the unreal composition of two mermaid skeletons found lying in an embrace. I pushed my face toward the glass and saw my breath touch it, tracing every bone with my gaze one by one.

On the surface, they were lovers, but what did it matter to me? In my interpretation, they were two women, a found family—a mentor and a protégé— succumbing to death in an embrace, exhausted by trying to interpret and make meaning of their relationship.

Emotional resonance traveled from the bottom of my heart up to my eyes, where tears started to flow. I damned Maxine for her dismissal of the project, for refusing to see the importance of this artwork to me. The dimness of that floor of the museum anonymized me. I was a member of an audience enjoying the recognition and release of being moved by a play. In a crowded room but privately, all to myself. I was one with the world but separate from it, lovingly bound to the complex inner workings of my consciousness.

Then, my oversight came flooding back. All the stories of the Mélusines began with a breaking of trust—the despair of someone beloved breaking a social contract. In every story, a secure woman had been slighted and despairingly consulted the underworld for answers. There, they faced what I had recognized before—a helpless deal—and disintegrated into the life of a monster upon failing the deal.

But the Mélusine wasn't a hopeless victim or a fair maiden doomed to ugliness. The Mélusines shared the commonality of multi-dimensional beings, so betrayed they were willing to engage in a deal with the devil. I sought the devil when Maxine betrayed me. Maxine sought the devil when I betrayed her. My version of the devil was the dark side of magic. Her version was human scorn, the worst punishment of all.

The uglier I looked, the closer I got to my true form. I didn't know how it would feel or what it would look like, but my yearning for it grew stronger every day, and my reflection grew stranger. The physical collapse that frightened others thrilled me. I wasn't dying. I was molting, shedding the constraints of human flesh to emerge as something perpetual.

Her death lorded over my life. In suicide, she'd risen above the power of her instincts and chosen an existence of true darkness. The real sense of darkness. The sort of darkness deprived of sensation. The kind of darkness that was so empty it wasn't even black. Her self-control prevailed above mine, untethered to fight or flight.

With my forehead still to the glass, drips of tears

making their own addition to the installation, I saw the truth in the embracing skeletons. They weren't just lovers or rivals—they were both victims and monsters, mentors and betrayers, each making the other what they became, just as Maxine and I had done.

I imagined the chicken and the egg forming a rotating order. A chicken lays the egg, the egg births a chicken, and the chicken lays the egg, and the egg births the chicken. An infinite reincarnation, pointing nowhere but to itself. A reality in which every solution was nothing more than a complicated answer. One that required too much backstory to decide on anything at all. A reality of *um*.

ACT III: SCENE III

I had my answer. I faltered back down the shambled cobblestone path back to the hotel. I took one large, final inhale of the quilt and the pillows that had absorbed my every odor. I lifted the bouquet of winter jasmine to my nose. Even in death, the scent embedded itself into my chest and mind. Triumphant. I took the small bottle of blood and made my way to the lake.

Lake Annecy was the most extravagant scene work I'd ever seen. I marveled at the set around me. The carousel lights from town reflected through the spinning animals like shadow puppets. Global tourists and Parisian weekenders enjoyed their vacations. Some came to ski, some stopped as a detail en route to Rome or Geneva, and others, like me, arrived for Annecy.

The sky was darkening, the carousel lights growing brighter. I ventured along the path into darker terrain, a cold, navy, hilly labyrinth where reflections of light disappeared with every step. Darkness and breath were all I had. I pressed the bouquet and the vial to my chest, basking in it. The world became empty, without furniture, lights, or sound cues.

Only one character needed a wretched little twenty-three-year-old who had all but turned to dust. Evil roiled inside like an unstoppable force, desperate to escape life as it was.

I owned this body first. I built this house and knew I needed to sell. I stood on the shore of the lake in an unknown location, unremarkable and untraceable, nobody in the world knowing where I was. Nobody missed me. I cried across the water, the same question I asked myself in the bathroom in Chicago. *Have you been here this whole time?*

I wanted to give everything so I could forget my human passions. My unending love for Maxine made me suffer, and suffer, and suffer. I tried to rip the skin off my body, knowing it would never bring her back to me. I had no guilt for placing evil between us. The real evil was our missed opportunity for something different. Where was my life with her? Where had it gone? I felt it in my heart like an old memory to reach back on. But the fact of the matter was I never had any time with her in the first place.

Forget all of this! I screamed. *Fuck you!* I scraped my fingernails in the sand, reaching for anything to answer what I'd lost. I was losing rationale, thrown into what felt like a holding area. I drooled and twitched, noticing then that everything was a prop.

Metaphor was gone. The world was a creation. The Earth was a ball of clay compacted by enormous hands. The planet still had carpet stuck to it. Popcorn crumbs in it. Feathers from the boa of a little girl in her first play. I forgot every memory as soon as it came to me. Gone was my childhood, detailed with the cheers from football fields, and leather boots.

Gone were the patios, the sizzling scents of steak fajitas, the cast irons full of queso, the ramekins of salsa. I forgot all the Spanglish I knew, all the hands I'd held, all the pining. My brain was a tabula rasa with no family, no lovers, no heart-to-hearts, void of connection. Dementia took over in every way but one: Maxine and her despicable, infinite well of knowledge and our shared pain.

The further I drifted from the physical presence of Maxine, the more I reasoned with her. I saw myself in her, our images becoming nearly indistinguishable.

I began to wish for a life I couldn't remember but still held the feeling of it. I forgot about theatre. With pain in my heart, I hoped for a life at the tip of my tongue. Years of collaboration and discussion. Harmless gatherings. I pined unconsciously for normalcy, hanging onto my values by a faint thread.

An ideal version of a playwriting residency put itself together in the emptiness of my head. I wanted a cohort to challenge me, bury itself in history with me, and scavenge for meaning in the way only artists can. I collapsed in a haze of confused awe.

In the distance of the sky, I watched a supernova. I interpreted it as the death of my life on Earth. Then, a quake. Tectonic plates I'd previously described as angry opened like grand gates. As they opened, the complexity of reality broke. Simplicity, plain as day. No more questions.

My human eyes adjusted to see beyond the physical plane.

A castle appeared at the bottom of the lake through the widening crack. From open windows, a swirl of slender, nearly two-foot-long water vipers twisted out and circulated their way closer to me in a hypnotic spiral.

People didn't exist, but if anyone rushed to find me, they'd see blankness. Quiet water and the familiarity of nighttime.

I kept the vial and the flowers to my chest and waded into the cold water. It felt painfully cold on my ankles, then my knees. The mountains surrounded me, every peak visible in the clear sky. I sighed. How nice it was to see the universe again after months of rain. The dried winter jasmine crumbled in my hand as I swam deeper. The separation of land and water grew indistinct.

As the void sucked me in, my strength revitalized, my gray hair shifted back to its original, brassy color, my hands softened and reshaped my hips and glutes and arms. Months before, I would have dropped the vial into the abyss, swam back to shore, and spread out on a rock to dry until sunrise. But I couldn't retreat to the familiarity of my youth. Instead, I shapeshifted into an unrecognizable thing.

Momentarily conscious of my resentment and self-satisfaction. Sick of it. Sick of it all. Sick of the suffering. I wasn't a victim of my tragedy. I was fearless in the face of it. I knew something was past life on Earth, and I was right. I relented to my decision and set my mind on the power Maxine had found, resisting the urge to fight and fight. I surrendered to float in the water on my back, facing up toward the sky.

The lake water was replaced with black scarves. The dark fabric stretched across the ceiling, bearing fiber optic stars. All of life was fabric—every bit of it. I came to destiny by my own accord, unwinding into what I refused to accept as the unknown. I had seen it, so I knew. I was timeless and would never get lost to history. My soul would never go to storage. I trusted it.

My experience became a myth of its own—a befallen heroine chased reconnection with artistry in the lesser-known Venice of the Alps nearly a year after cursing her respected teacher.

I felt her there all around me. My thighs went rigid, my ribs felt like they were falling off me one by one, and my throat got so tight it throbbed, almost without thinking. The fear exhilarated me from the wilderness I'd carried for so long. Feeling like fate told me to, I tapped into it, wishing that whoever would listen would understand my clarity. Deprived of empathy, I sweat more in the cold water, every ring of my existence falling apart.

A vision of a false, impossible future, where years had passed, and I gave her a call. *Any time*, just as she promised:

MAXINE

Hey, Texas. I didn't expect to see this Dallas number on
my phone again.

I squeezed my mouth together to restrain the flood of emotion. Then, I started laughing and couldn't stop. I was so excited, tumbling into total confusion. Then, she started laughing, too.

MAXINE
Corey, what's funny?

COREY

I can't believe I'm hearing your voice. Hi.

MAXINE

Thank you for calling.

COREY

I didn't know if you still wanted space or—

MAXINE

No. I'm happy you called me. Howdy.

COREY

Howdy.

I sat for a while in my fantasy, listening to her breath through the phone's silence. Maybe Maxine and I could have been the opposite of fate; room for a resolution to be just the start of it.

Stars lowered above me on visible strings. A chain lowered down, holding the moon. When Tony Kushner wrote *Angels in America*, he said he wanted the lines the angels flew on to be apparent to the audience. I marveled at all of it. Back at the center of people, silhouettes of marionettes filled the townhome windows—children and parents curled up in their living rooms, petting their cats and dogs. The chickens were still out making a racket. Didn't they ever sleep?

Playgoers were more willing to take a story at face value and relish in the magic when the lights went down. In the real world, they were stupidly committed to questioning, unaware that ingenuity, as they understood it, was a fallacy.

I thought of those skeletons in their eternal embrace. How even in death, they remained locked together, their bones intertwined like lovers or enemies or both. Maxine and I would share that fate—not in a museum case, but in the dark waters of Lake Annecy. Two Mélusines, two betrayers, two monsters who chose their endings.

At the center of the hole of spiraling snakes, a three-dimensional object floated up—an unremarkable seashell attached to a delicate gold chain. This light, tan, and periwinkle shell that washed beside me wasn't some sinister signal—it was only a child's plaything. A signal not to take things so seriously.

I wished I could go back in time to tell my younger self the necklace was coming to me—that during every painful moment, it drifted closer. I looped it over my head and floated, patiently waiting for the monster to feed. May the gods have mercy on my soul.

Blackout.

The End of Act III.

The End.

Acknowledgments

Thank you to my mentors whom I love and don't want to place curses on. Thank you to CLASH Books—Christoph, Leza, and Kaitlyn—for taking me on and kicking ideas around along the way.

Thank you to collaborators who read and gave feedback as I went: Alicia Brooks, Angela Capovani, Autumn Christian, James Charlesworth, Juliana Lopez, and others. Thank you to Rose Pacult for a new friendship that was integral to this process. Thank you to my mom, dad, brother, sister, and in-laws for all the encouragement.

In Texas: Thank you to Plano Children's Theatre, McKinney Youth Theatre, and the drama department of Hebron High School for encouraging children to pursue the arts. Most especially, thank you to Dusty Thompson and Cade Butler for letting me try out playwriting. It was fun! I dropped everything and chased it.

In Chicago: Thank you to The Theatre School at DePaul University, to Lookingglass Theatre Company for my first official job in new play development, to all the storefront theatres that have given me reign to book a space and do weird stuff, and to everyone who's extended opportunities so I can work and play. Thank you to the actors, directors, and designers I've worked with for imprinting the idea that writing a play is a collaborative art and not some insular, lonely endeavor.

Thank you to the Creative Writing and Publishing MFA at DePaul, who encouraged my hybridity and got me thinking: *Maybe a book could be a play.* And thank you to my students, who inspire me right on schedule every week.

Most importantly, thank you to my husband Andy, who makes me black coffee during happy hour every night so that I can finish this book, and to my son Augie, who cues up "calming music" during it.

About the Author

Photo by Jewells Santos

Caroline Macon Fleischer is an author and theatre artist. Her first novel, *The Roommate*, was a Kindle thriller bestseller in the summer of 2022. In theatre, she's worked in many capacities for companies including Lookingglass Theatre Company, Chicago Children's Theatre, Chicago Dramatists, and more. She is also a member of Poems While You Wait, a collective of poets and their typewriters that writes original poetry on demand. She teaches at Loyola University and lives in Chicago with her husband and son. Find her online @caromacon and www.caromacon.com.

Also by CLASH Books

CHARCOAL

Garrett Cook

LES FEMMES GROTESQUES

Victoria Dalpe

DARRYL

Jackie Ess

VIOLENT FACULTIES

Charlene Elsby

LIFE OF THE PARTY

Tea Hačić-Vlahović

BURN FORTUNE

Brandi Homan

BELOW THE GRAND HOTEL

Cat Scully

ON SUBMISSION

Michael J. Seidlinger

CATHERINE THE GHOST

Kathe Koja